T0113612

The Saviours of Forest City

"A story for all boys and girls"

Arturo Lopez

authorHOUSE®

AuthorHouse™
1663 Liberty Drive
Bloomington, IN 47403
www.authorhouse.com
Phone: 833-262-8899

Published by AuthorHouse 01/13/2022

ISBN: 978-1-6655-4954-7 (sc)
ISBN: 978-1-6655-4959-2 (e)

Library of Congress Control Number: 2022900939

Print information available on the last page.

Any people depicted in stock imagery provided by Getty Images are models, and such images are being used for illustrative purposes only.
Certain stock imagery © Getty Images.

This book is printed on acid-free paper.

The team rises

Contents

Prologue

The years were 2075 and 2076.

A superhero by the name of Bird became the first real-life superhero mentioned in the news but was never seen by the public. In the news, it was revealed it was a he and looked and sounded like an actual sparrow. He was once a famous superhero in the year 2075 and 2076, there were lots of merchandise including comics about him. On two Halloween nights, boys, and girls would always dress up like him and act all heroic. Rather than being feared by children, he was looked up to by them as a heroic symbol. Something that would always protect their large and extraordinary city, Forest City.

However and unfortunately, every superhero must always have a supervillain. For Bird, it was the devil of Forest City "The White Magician" It was revealed the devil was taller in size than Bird's age and that it might have been a different species. The devil had all kinds of powers. In the news, The White Magician had the power of moving things by using its hands, going into people's minds as well as reading them, turning itself invisible, having lots of magical abilities, and finally pausing the fabric of time. It was also rumored to eat people.

Most people wouldn't believe in The Bird or The White Magician. They thought it was nothing but a gimmick. Every time the Bird fought evil foes like The White Magician, it would always be number #1 on trending as well as the most talked-about streaming and iPhones. YouTube would be the third most talked of The Bird, his foes including The White Magician itself. The Bird and his enemies were everywhere around the world including Forest City.

However and sadly on the Christmas of 2076, The Bird was no longer saving people, people would always get beat up by criminals as well as getting murdered by murders. Some of the people truly miss The Bird and his heroic actions. As for The White Magician, it was never heard of ever again.

In the year 2076, the father of Andrew Luck adopted an eleven-year-old girl named Sophia Smith. Sophia Smith had dark orange hair as well as light orange eyes. Once Sophia Smith met her new brother Andrew Luck, Andrew greeted her nicely while Sophia was too shy to greet him. Thankfully as the days went by, she became more of a social person with her family but not with other people other than her teachers. She would always get bullied by some kids her age, Andrew would always tell her to ignore them. However, and sadly, even though she would try her best to ignore them, in the end, she would always fight them. She could give hard punches at them but sadly she could always get a black eye or her teeth knocked out by them. Everything would always be the same for the two Lucks and Sophia Smith until something magnificent occurred...

I

The Field Trip

The year is now 2077.

Inside 123 Pine Street, Andrew and his father were singing happy birthday to Sophia Smith; she turned twelve years old today on July 15. It was a small cake since there were only three people in the kitchen. Once they finished singing the birthday song to Sophia, Sophia thanked the two and hugged them with a smile.

"Here's your gift Sophia," said Andrew Luck, who had Sophia's gift in his hands. The box was all orange and white.

"Thank you brother," Sophia Smith replied back to him, who now had the present in her hands. Once she unwrapped her present, she saw that there was something small inside of it, "A book?"

"Not just a book," He told her, "this used to be one of my favorite books when I was five years old,"

"The Wonderful Wizard of Oz?"

"Exactly Sophia,"

"Is it good?"

"Better than the movie,"

"I haven't even seen the movie,"

"Don't,"

"Isn't that a classic?"

"Not for me Sophia,"

"Trust him, Sophia, this book is good," said her father.

"How old is this book exactly?" she asked them curiously.

"177 years old," replied Andrew.

"God, that's old,"

"It may be old and outdated," Andrew told her, "but it's still a classic story,"

"I guess I'll read it, Andrew"

"That's great Sophia," he replied.

"Who's ready for some cake?" asked the father.

"I'm always ready for cake," said Andrew.

"What kind of question is that?" asked Sophia, "Of course, I would want some chocolate cake,"

After eating the entire cake, Sophia and Andrew went back to bed while their father was taking a shower.

"Pssst…"

Andrew woke up and saw on his right his sister, Sophia all woke up.

"What do you want, Sophia?" Andrew muttered to her.

"Have you ever had a crush before?" Sophia asked him curiously.

"Why do you ask?"

"Because…"

"Who is he?"

"Oh, shut up,"

"No please, tell me,"

"There's this really small, cute boy in my middle school,"

"What's his name?"

"I never asked him,"

"Why not?"

"I'm too nervous to talk to boys, Andrew,"

"What about me?"

"Who isn't family,"

"Oh,"

"What should I do, Andrew?" she asked him curiously.

"When I was your age, I used to be shy in front of girls," he told her, "You want to know when I faced my fears?"

"How did you face your fears?"

"When I bumped into a cute girl,"

"What was her name?"

"Olivia Wind,"

"What a beautiful name,"

"I know,"

"What was she like?"

"She had cute blonde hair and beautiful brown eyes," he told her, "she was also fun and adventurous."

"What do you mean?"

"I and her would always have amazing adventures in Forest City along with another girl, her best friend,"

"What was her name?"

"Katren Leaf,"

"Did you have a crush on her as well?"

Andrew gave Sophia a look and told her, "Just because I meet another girl doesn't mean I had a crush on her,"

"Just asking," she told him, "what kind of adventures did you do with them?"

"I, Olivia, and Katren would always go to the forest and many more places whenever we felt bored,"

"Nice," she told him, "tell me more about Olivia,"

"We were first friends in the beginning," he told her, "however, one day me and her became more than friends. We started a relationship,"

"How come I've never seen her before?"

"Years before we adopted you, we got into a fight."

"What were you two fighting about?"

"It was about..." he stood as still as a statue while Sophia gave out a confused expression on her face until Andrew finally told her, "it's not important, what's important is you shouldn't be shy in front of boys. Face your fears, and when you do then perhaps you and him might become a relationship."

"Thanks, brother,"

"No problem sister," he told her, "now let's go to sleep before our dad hears us talking to each other again,"

"Okay,"

Sophia was now asleep while Andrew stayed awake for a good minute until he fell asleep.

July 19th

Today is a special day for Sophia Smith. Today was the last field trip for her summer school. Sophia was on a bus that could fly with its technological wheels. Sophia Smith was sitting all by herself, she could see her small crush from three seats away. Sophia and her classmates were about to go to the most famous building in the city "L.A.B.S." L.A.B.S. is one of the most famous companies in Forest City. It was created by Karen Labs and has also created many other L.A.B.S.-related buildings from schools to stores. Andrew was one of the lucky students who attended L.A.B.S. Middle School as well as attending L.A.B.S. High School. The schools would only allow kids who are gifted with brilliant minds like Karen Labs, herself.

Sophia and many other students saw the "L.A.B.S." building. It was the tallest building in the entire world.

"Everyone get back into your seats!" cried the bus driver, "We're about to go down!"

Everyone but Sophia got back to their seats; Sophia never left her seat in the first place. Once the bus flew down onto the parking lot, every student including Sophia got out of the bus. All the students but Sophia wanted to go inside and explore the building, however, the teacher would have to tell every student the rules. From never getting lost to touching anything. After she was done explaining the rules, she told every student to follow her, and they began following her including Sophia.

Inside the building was amazing! It was filled with many technologies such as robots and inventions and had many floors. The building was indeed enormous. Every student but Sophia was amazed because Sophia didn't much care for science or technology. She was more of a sports and gymnastics girl.

"Hello my name is Selina Labs, daughter of Karen Labs," she told the students, "and welcome to L.A.B.S. I'll be your guide for the tour today, any questions before we start?"

Lots of students except Sophia raised their hands as high as they could. Selina picked the first hand she saw and told her, "Yes,"

"Where is Karen Labs?" she asked her curiously, "Is she here today?"

"My mother isn't here today, she's too busy,"

"Oh," she replied.

After answering their questions, the tour had now begun. After many minutes of walking on many floors. They were now in the radiation room. It was filled with a ton of toxic waste; it almost looked like a nuclear plant from the inside.

"In here, we have where we create our nuclear weapons,"

Every student but Sophia was amazed since Sophia didn't much care for nuclear weapons. Suddenly, an explosion erupted from beneath another floor and made a quick shake around the building. The shake was so strong, Sophia accidentally fell down and landed on toxic waste. She wasn't the only one to accidentally fell down as well as landing on toxic waste, a small boy fell down at the same time Sophia did, however, he was holding his bucket of slime. Sophia tried swimming back up as she could, but she couldn't breathe and later passed out from all the toxic waste consuming her body. As for the boy, he too tried to swim up, however, he accidentally ate his slime and began choking, and later passed out from both the slime and toxic waste.

Meanwhile, it was now lunchtime in L.A.B.S. High School, Andrew was watching a YouTube video about L.A.B.S. when suddenly he decided to look at the news and saw that the L.A.B.S. building was in flames, and many metal pieces were falling apart. Andrew then used his head on trying to find his sister, only to find out that both she and a small boy were now beneath the toxic waste. Andrew gave out a terrified expression and ran as fast as he could outside the school. With no one around to see him, he quickly turned into a large sparrow creature and began to fly as high as he could into the clouds; hoping to avoid flying cars. He flew as fast as he could with superspeed and was now inside of his basement. He quickly opened a wardrobe, grabbed his hazmat suit and flew outside his house, and began flying to L.A.B.S.

Once he was finally inside of the "L.A.B.S." building, he quickly flew as fast as he could into the radiation room. He quickly flew to the right and grabbed his sister Sophia. He then quickly flew to the left and grabbed the small boy on his left feather. He quickly got out of the building and approached the city's hospital as fast as he could. He slowly put them down onto the ground and flew up into the nearest building. Once he was there, he saw a doctor grabbing Sophia and a nurse grabbing the small boy. They both ran as quickly as they could inside of the hospital, Andrew gave out a smile and began flying back into his summer school. Luckily, nobody noticed from both above and below.

II

The Reveal of A Superhero

A man in orange clothing was walking into his boss's office.
"What is it Michael?" she asked him curiously.
"I have some bad news for you,"
"What is it?"
"He can't complete the machine without any radiation,"
"Why didn't you get radiation when you had the chance?"
"I didn't know we needed it in the first place,"

She began to laugh as crazily as she could, and told him, "Oh Michael," she then turned her floating chair around, "you are as dumb as a donkey for not thinking about that...!" the tall yet small girl he was talking to is a rabbit wearing a large top hat, a fancy suit, a long cape, soft white gloves, and finally pointy black shoes. Her eyes were as red as blood. She also had a white dot on the bottom of her eyes, she had them for both on opposite sides. Her teeth were as small and sharp as monster teeth. She had a small nose, which had whiskers beneath the nose.

"I might be seventeen, but I could still kick your behind." she told him, "Even with your flaming powers,"

"I understand, White Magician," he told her, "please forgive me, my boss,"

"Forgiving you would just be as dumb as you,"

He had no words to say to her, however, he couldn't even look back at her.

"Aw, does the flaming man want to go back home and cry to his mama?" she told him, "Well guess what, your mama's dead in Hell!"

"Again, I'm sorry,"

"Oh, you sorry big guy? You sorry?" she told him, "Well hurray for you because no one gives a darn about you or your life. You must go back to L.A.B.S. and retrieve the radiation, you did well when you bombed it,"

"Yes my lord,"

"Oh, and if you fail me again," she told him, "I will cut off your head with my claws and wear it as a mask for this year's Halloween! As for the rest of your body, I'll just eat it,"

She began to laugh as crazily as she could and give out a grin on her face.

"I understand, Miss Magician,"

"Oh please Michael, Miss Magician was my mother's last name if she were still alive,"

"I understand boss,"

"I understand... I understand...!" she mocked him, "Shut up with that, and bring me the radiation!"

"Yes, White Magician," He began leaving while The White Magician grinned and once again laughed as crazily as she could to herself. Once she stopped laughing she told herself, "I wonder in the meantime, I could find an old friend. I mean, after all, he is back in the news," she saw in an image in one of her many televisions; revealing what looked to be a large sparrow from a camera back at the "L.A.B.S." building. Her grin was now as larger than her face and she once more laughed to herself as crazily as she could, "It has begun old friend," She then pulled out her large tongue and began licking her own dry lips.

Once Sophia woke up and gasped, she noticed she was in a hospital bed. She also noticed she was now wearing some sort of blue clothing since her normal clothing was gone. A nurse walked into the room and noticed her awake, "Hello," she told Sophia.

"Hi," she replied, "where the heck am I?"

"You're in the hospital,"

"Why am I here?"

The nurse was as silent and still as a statue. Sophia then cried to her, "I said, why the heck am I here!?" After a long moment of silence, the nurse told Sophia she was laying on the ground and was picked up by a doctor, who later helped her for a week. Sophia was as a shock as ever, looked at the nurse, and asked her where the doctor went.

"He's calling your father,"

"What's he telling him?"

"He's informing him about your health and some concerns,"

"What about them?"

The nurse was as silent and still as a statue once more until Sophia cried to her, "Just gosh darn tell me!"

"He used an x-ray and scanned that your body has some sort of radiation inside of your body," she replied.

"Cancer?"

"No, not that,"

"Then what is it?"

"He doesn't know yet," she told her, she then grabbed a needle "so if you please just stay still and calm while I inject this needle into your arm,"

"Why!?" she asked her curiously.

"We need you asleep for an operation,"

"An operation?"

"Just hold still,"

"Stay away from me!" she cried to the nurse, she pulled her hand up and made a stop hand signal as quickly as she could. Suddenly, the nurse was pushed into the wall. She then screamed as loud as she could since her spine was now broken. A gasp came out of Sophia's mouth, and suddenly her skin was turning all green and was as bright as a lantern. She quickly got out of bed and ran as quickly out as she could. Every time a doctor or nurse saw her, they were just freaked out on seeing a green girl. Once she got out of the hospital, she ran as quickly as she could in the right direction at midnight. She hoped to get back home as safely as she could.

Meanwhile, in 123 Pine Street, Andrew and his father were having a discussion in the living room.

"Andrew, you know how I feel when you use your powers,"

"I know dad," he told him, "but I had to in order to save my sister,"

"What you did was right, and did you make sure nobody saw you flying?"

"Don't worry, nobody saw me,"

The father's iPhone suddenly rang. Once he answered it, he listened and then dropped his phone and was staying as still as a statue.

"Dad are you alright?"

"Use your powers now,"

"Why?"

"She's gone,"

Andrew looked down and gave out a horrified expression. He then used his mind. Once he did, he stopped and told his father, "I'll see you later," He then used his super-speed to get outside of his home, transformed back into a sparrow, and flew as fast as he could.

"I hope nothing bad happens to her," he thought to himself.

Sophia was now running into the forest; she was lost. She didn't know where else to go and was worried until she saw something right next to her shadow. It was another shadow; it wasn't the shadow of a tree but rather of a person. Sophia was confused until she felt somebody hugging her as well as pulling her up. She then used her hands to hit the person's face, and once she got back down she ran as fast as she could into the right side of the forest. She could hear footsteps from behind her, she decided to run ten times faster, as best as she could since back in P.E. class she would always be the fastest runner in her class. Suddenly, Sophia tripped on a small tree branch and fell down onto the rough ground. She didn't mind the dirt on her, since she would always play basketball outside. Once she turned behind, she could see the image of a man with orange clothing.

"What the heck do you want?" she asked him curiously.

"Sophia Smith, you're coming with me,"

"How do you…" She gave out an angry look and told the man in orange, "Listen, sir, you better back off, or I will kick you in your meatballs!"

The man laughed a little, and suddenly his whole body was now in flames, and the only thing she saw was his skeleton. Sophia gave out a horrified expression and cried out the words, "What the heck!?" The man was about to grab Sophia, which she gasped until something super punched him into a tree. Sophia looked at the flaming person and was confused until she turned back and saw the image of a tall sparrow.

"What is going on with the world today?" she thought to herself, curiously.

"Sophia, we need to leave!"

"Who are you!?"

"You know who I am,"

"No, I..." Sophia then looked at his brown eyes and recognized them, "Andrew?"

"Shhh..." he shushed her, "you can't say my name, not in front of the bad guy,"

"Sorry," she told him in a silent tone, "it's just WHAT THE HECK!?"

"Shhh..." He shushed her while covering up her mouth.

Suddenly, the man woke up and was about to attack both of them. Luckily, Andrew noticed and told Sophia, "Look out!" He pushed her onto the right side and received a flaming punch from a man and was pushed into a tree; breaking his back.

"Andrew!" she cried to him. She gave an angry look, stood up, and was about to approach the man and give him a fist until he stopped her fist.

"How can I not feel any pain?" she thought to herself, curiously, "Maybe it's because of my body being all green and shiny,"

Suddenly, the man grabbed Sophia's arm and began walking in the opposite direction.

"Let me go!" She began punching him as many times as she could until she pulled out her hand and suddenly the flaming man was pushed into another tree; only this time he felt more pain than he did before.

"Did I do that!?" she thought to herself curiously, "What is really going on,"

The man opened his eyes and was about to attack her until suddenly a splash of water pushed and got rid of all his fiery body. Sophia looked on her right and saw a man whose body is made out of water with a belt that had a buckled "W" and a woman whose body was made out of plants. She was more surprised at what she was seeing and told the two curiously, "Who the heck are you two?"

"The Waterman,"

"Plant-Woman,"

The man woke up and was then super punched by Plant-Woman on his left cheek, which made him spit out one of his teeth. He turned back into his fiery form and flew off to the sky. Sophia looked at the two and then looked at her brother Andrew all beaten, she gasped and told the two, "That's my brother! Help him, please," The two looked at each other and both nodded to her. They grabbed him, Andrew then noticed her sister being all right as well as the two people caring him. He asked who they were, and the two replied with their names.

"Well that's nice," said Andrew.

"Andrew!" cried Sophia, who ran to him and gave him a hug, "Please be alright!"

"Don't worry Sophia," he told her, "I can heal pretty fast!" His bones got back together and he was able to move again. He then grabbed Sophia, stepped two times backward and thanked the two for what they had done, and told them, "Now if you excuse us, me and my sister need to go back home,"

"We understand," replied The Waterman.

"Great,"

"Are we really going home, Andrew?" Sophia asked him curiously.

"Yes,"

"Oh thank god," She then looked at the two people and told them, "Thank you,"

They both gave a smile while Andrew flew away with Sophia. Sophia looked down and could see the forest, she then saw the entire city. Sophia was amazed at what she was seeing; she wasn't inside of her father's vehicle, she was flying with Andrew, and she could feel the clouds as well.

Meanwhile back with the bad guys, Michael finally went back to their hideout.

"You're late as usual," he told him.

"I'm sorry,"

"Next time please don't be," He turned his head towards him, revealing the face of a talking pencil.

"I'm sorry Professor Pencil,"

"You're just lucky I'm not her,"

"Indeed,"

"Did you get the girl?"

"No,"

"Oh, if I was the boss," he told him, "I would have forgiven you, but since I'm not, I could only say this to you, good luck with her,"

"Thank you,"

"No problem," he told him, "now be a man and inform her of your failures,"

Michael then walked towards the enormous doors, opened them, and began walking into the room. Before he could say anything to his boss, she told him, "Hello again, Michael,"

"Hello, boss,"

"Do you have the girl?"

"No,"

"Ha!" she laughed, "I knew it. Normally I would always want to threaten you, but now…"

Suddenly, Michael felt pain inside of his body as if somebody was controlling him. He suddenly flew up and was confused until he noticed this was the work of his boss "The White Magician" Suddenly he flew down again and was quickly pushed by her, "You miserable piece of flames!" Suddenly, she was now behind him and punched him behind his head, Michael let out a scream of agony and could then feel something crushing his body; he looked down and saw that The White Magician was bear-hugging him. He could barely breathe and felt his bones almost break.

"I'm sorry!"

"Sorry doesn't help!" She then pushed her hands as tightly as she could into his back; Michael let out another scream of agony, "Now it's time for you to die!"

"But it wasn't my fault!"

"Who was it then you flaming idiot!"

"A SPARROW!"

She then gave a realized look and stopped hugging him, he fell down onto the floor. He could barely breathe.

"Was that all?" she asked him curiously.

"No, there was also a man whose body was made out of the water," he told her, "and a woman whose body was made out of plants,"

"Michael, I want you to find them!"

"What!?"

"Before you even say anything," she told him, "if you don't get both the girl and the bird, I will give you one of the biggest bearhugs I have ever given and once I crush your spine, I will eat your entire body while I keep your spine in my collection,"

"Yes, White Magician," he then looked down.

"Aw, do you want to cry?" she told him, "Well don't! Go to their home and grab both of them!"

"What if the little girl has parents?"

"Kill them!" she cried to him, "I don't care!" She slapped him on his right cheek.

Meanwhile, in 123 Pine Street, Andrew and Sophia were now outside of their front door. Sophia knocked on it, and they could hear footsteps from downstairs. Once the door was opened, their father looked at them and gave both of them a big hug.

"I miss you daddy!" she cried to him.

"I miss you too sweetie," he then told Andrew, "Thank you, Andrew,"

"There's something we need to tell you,"

The three were now inside the living room. The father asked Andrew, "You're telling me there are still more superheroes like you?"

"I don't know if they're superheroes," he replied.

"They did just saved our lives, Andrew," she told him, "and also you're Bird!?"

"Yes, I am Bird,"

"Why didn't either of you two tell me?"

"We were afraid," replied Andrew.

"I might have been afraid at first," she told him, "but you saved my life from that awful man, Andrew,"

"With some help from unexpected people,"

Sophia chuckled. She looked at both of them and told them, "Sorry… but seriously, I'm not afraid, Andrew."

"You're not?"

"Of course not," she told him, "you're my brother, and I'll always love you," She then gave him a hug. He hugged her back while the father smiled.

III

The House In Flames

"Goodnight Sophia," said Andrew.

"Goodnight Andrew," said Sophia.

Thirty minutes had passed...

"Pssst..."

Andrew woke up and told her, "We really shouldn't be talking at night time, Sophia,"

"I know it's just why did you quit?"

"What?"

"Why did you quit?"

No words came out of his mouth, Andrew was all silent. Sophia was about to say something until Andrew replied, "Because of her,"

"Who?"

"The White Magician,"

"The White Magician was real too?"

"They're all real,"

"What did she do to you?"

"Do you remember Olivia Wind?"

"Yes,"

"One day in 2076 in December," he told her, "The White Magician took Olivia, and told me to meet her in an abandoned house in the city."

"What happened next?"

"Then, she killed her,"

"Andrew, I'm so sorry,"

"It's alright,"

"What about Katren?"

"The White Magician also took Katren but spared her,"

"Why did she spared her?"

"Because I told her too," he told her, "and she agreed,"

"Did you defeat her?"

"No,"

"What do you mean, no?"

"What I mean is she almost killed me once we fought,"

"Don't you have healing powers?"

"I do," he told her, "but she was my weakness,"

"In your silly fictional stories," she told him, "a superhero always has a weakness,"

"Exactly,"

"How did you make it out of there alive?"

"She spared me,"

"Why did she spare you?"

"Because she was also in love with me,"

"What?"

"You heard me,"

"How could a monster love you?"

"I was one of her sidekicks,"

"Sidekick?"

"Back then," he told her, "she used to go by the name of The Mind Reader."

"The Mind Reader?" she told him, "That's a really ridiculous name,"

He chuckled, and told her, "I thought that too,"

"What was she like as The Mind Reader?"

"She was brave, smart, and strong,"

"What else?"

"Me and her would always fight the forces of evil," he told her, "from criminals to murders, normal people and super people,"

"Were they hard to fight?"

"Hmmm…?"

"The supervillains,"

"Always,"

"Why did she stop becoming a good person?"

"After a mission of ours gone horribly wrong," he told her, "The Mind Reader started feeling a bit odd about herself, almost as if she were crazy…"

"How did you survive from her?"

"I just got lucky," he told her, "I was just one of her sidekicks after all, The Wooden Sparrow"

"The Wooden Sparrow?"

"My old name,"

"Oh," she said, "you had a name before Bird… how come nobody's seen them before?"

"They were hidden from society from the government and Freedom," he told her.

"The agency?"

"Yes,"

"Alright…" she replied, "how did you get your superpowers?"

"It's a long story,"

"I don't care if it is,"

"Tell you what," he told her, "let's first go to sleep, and then I'll tell you about it first thing in the morning, deal?"

"Deal."

"Goodnight Sophia,"

"Goodnight Andrew,"

One hour later, Sophia woke up after she heard an odd sound from down the living room. It sounded like a piece of broken glass on the ground.

"Pssst…"

Andrew woke up all exhausted, looked at Sophia, and told her, "Didn't I tell you that I was going to tell you about it first thing in the morning?"

"It's not that Andrew," she told him, "I heard something coming from downstairs."

"What was it?"

"It sounded like a piece of broken glass,"

"It's probably your imagination,"

"Trust me, Andrew," he told her, "it's not,"

"Fine, but I'll check it out,"

"Can I come with you?"

"No way," he told her, "the older sibling always has to protect his or her siblings,"

"But,"

"No buts young lady,"

"Alright," she muttered to him. Sophia folded her arms.

"Sophia," he told her.

"Just go and see what's going on downstairs,"

Andrew got up, walked towards the bedroom door, opened it, and walked slowly down the stairs. Once Sophia heard Andrew taking his last step, she could hear him all confused, and then the sound of a punch. Andrew fell down the small stairs, got back up, transformed back into a sparrow, and was fighting whoever was downstairs.

"What is going on?" she thought to herself curiously. Sophia then got out of her bed and then began walking down the stairs; only to find Andrew fighting none other than the man, who was attacking them in the forest. He was in his fiery form while Andrew tried avoiding the fireballs he was throwing at him.

"Andrew!" she cried as loudly as she could.

Once he noticed her, he yelled to her, "What are you doing here!?"

"I was just…" she told him, "Um… I, um…"

"There you are!" cried the man.

"Oh no, you're not!" cried Andrew, who flew directly at him and pushed him into the couch.

"Sophia, Andrew," yelled the father, who was out of his room, "what's going… oh my god!"

"Protect Sophia!" he told him, "While I take care of this fireman!"

"Sophia, come with me!" yelled her father.

No words came out of her mouth, Sophia looked at her father and looked back at Andrew and the flaming man. After a few minutes of thinking, Sophia closed both of her eyes and took a deep breath, and decided to run towards Andrew and the flaming man.

"Sophia!" cried her father.

Sophia then jumped and punched the flaming man in the face as hard as she could. Andrew saw, looked at Sophia, and told her, "What are you doing!?"

"Saving your life, Andrew!" she cried to him, "You think I'm just going to let my brother get hurt again by this mister flames?"

"I can heal!"

"Well, you weren't able to heal as fast as you could last time,"

Once the man opened both of his eyes, he grabbed both Sophia and Andrew by the throat, and cried to both of them, "You two are coming with me!"

"I don't think so flames!" cried the father, who had a fire extinguisher in his hands. Once he turned it on, it began spreading all over the man; making him get pushed through the window while both Andrew and Sophia fell down onto the couch.

"Are you two alright?" asked their father curiously.

"Yeah dad," replied Sophia.

"Same here dad," replied Andrew.

"Good, now let's run!"

The two then noticed the whole house was now on fire.

"Grab my hands!" cried Andrew.

Both his father and sister grabbed one hand from Andrew. Andrew then flew up as high as he could and hoped to land somewhere safe, in which nobody could see he was a large sparrow and that his sister's body was all green and shiny.

The man woke up, looked up in the sky, and shouted out loud to himself, "No!" He then punched the grass as hard as he could.

"IDIOT!" cried The White Magician, who was seeing him from a camera, "At least that idiot burned down that house," The White Magician gave a look until she noticed on one of her televisions the image of a slime boy running in the forest. She pushed her hands into her face all frustrated and said to herself, "Fine! I guess I'll give the flaming idiot one more chance," She grinned once more.

IV

The Slime-Boy In The Forest

"Where are we going, Andrew?" Sophia asked him curiously.

"The forest,"

"You mean where we met that flaming man?" she asked him curiously, "Why?"

"I think, I might know two people who know the answer,"

Once Andrew landed safely down onto the rough, dirty ground both his father and sister let go of him and then began following him. Once Sophia took her thirteen-step, she felt something soft and squishy on her right foot.

"Huh?" she thought to herself curiously, "Slime?"

It was light-green soft slime. Sophia then told Andrew and her father, "You guys, I think I found something," Once they looked at her, they noticed the slime.

"Slime?" Andrew asked.

"Ugh!" cried their father disgusted.

"It's alright dad," she told him, "nothing grosses me out,"

"Sophia, come closer," Andrew told her.

Once Sophia got closer, Andrew told her, "I need you to lift your right foot," Once she did, Andrew touched the slime and was examining it.

"Ugh!" cried their father disgusted, "Andrew, that's gross!"

"It's alright dad," said Sophia, "I think I know what Andrew's doing,"

"Thank you, Sophia," Once he finished examining the slime by sniffing it, he began sniffing something and gave out a look on his face, "We're not alone,"

"What do you mean we're not alone?" Sophia asked him curiously.

"Somebody's behind that tree,"

The two looked at the tree and noticed a leg made entirely out of the green slime.

"Who's there!?" cried Sophia, curiously.

They heard a gasp, and suddenly whatever it was ran away. They could see the back of its body.

"You scared it away, Sophia!" cried Andrew.

"I didn't mean to!"

"Come on!" he told them.

The three were running as fast as they could in order to approach the slime kid. The slime kid then tripped over a branch, and was crying to them, "Please don't hurt me!"

"Hurt you?" she asked him, curiously.

"We're not here to hurt you kid," Andrew told him.

Once he stopped sobbing, he looked at the three and told him, "You're not?" It was a boy made entirely out of slime, he was dripping slime all over his body. His eyes were, however, black with a white dot in the middle and its teeth were sharp. He also had four fingers as well as four toes.

"What the heck is that!?" Sophia asked her brother and father curiously and terrified.

"Sophia!" Andrew shouted to her, "Don't be rude,"

"I'm just saying, Andrew,"

Andrew gave out a heavy sigh, he looked at the slime kid and told him, "We're not here to hurt you kid," He pulled out his hand and smiled at him, "trust me." The slime kid grabbed his right hand as slowly as he could and got back up, "I know you,"

"You do?" Andrew asked the slime kid.

"You're him," he said, "Bird,"

"Oh," he replied, "that's correct… What's your name kid?"

"Slime-Boy,"

"No, I mean your real name,"

"I don't know,"

"Alright…?"

"He asked you a question, Slime-Boy!" she cried to him, "So tell him!"

"Sophia!" Andrew cried to her, "Be nice,"

"To that thing?" she shouted to him, "I don't think so!"

"Sophia!" shouted her father.

"Look at it!"

"What about your brother?" he asked her curiously.

"Please shut up," she muttered to him, "I don't want this thing to know who we are,"

"But he looks like a good kid,"

"A good kid?" she replied. She pointed at Slime-Boy while saying to both her father and brother, "That thing does not look like a good kid! It looks like a monster!"

"Sophia!" shouted Andrew.

"What?" she told him, "Look at it!"

"What about Waterman and Plant-Woman?"

"Hey!" she shouted to him, "They looked innocent and beautiful… this thing, however, looks like a frigging freak of nature,"

"Sophia!" cried, Andrew.

"No, she's right," said Slime-Boy.

"No, she's not," he told him, "you are innocent and beautiful as well,"

"How do you know?" he asked him curiously, "You don't even know me!"

"I might not," he told him, "but I know a good kid when I see one,"

"What do you want?" he asked him curiously.

"For starters," said Sophia, "why were you frigging spying on us you creep!"

"Sophia!" shouted Andrew.

"What!?" she shouted to him, "I just want to know,"

"I wasn't spying on you guys," he told them, "I was just hiding from you guys,"

"Why were you hiding?" asked Andrew, curiously.

"Because I was scared,"

"Scared of what?" Andrew asked him curiously.

"Looking at me,"

"You almost dodge a bullet there," muttered Sophia.

Andrew looked at Sophia and gave her a look. Sophia folded her arms while Andrew looked back at Slime-Boy and told him, "It's alright, nobody here but my sister is scared of you,"

"Really?" he asked him curiously.

"Really Slime-Boy," he told him.

Slime-Boy weep a tear on his right eye and gave him a big hug as well as a smile. Andrew hugged him back along with a smile.

Meanwhile back with the bad guys, after Michael got back from stealing clothing once more, he decided to go talk to Professor Pencil. Once he walked towards him, he was about to say something to him until Professor Pencil told him, "You didn't get both the bird and girl, did you?"

"How can you honestly tell?"

"Brilliant mind, Michael," he replied, "brilliant mind,"

"She is going to kill me," he told him, "should I attack her before she kills me?"

"Oh, I don't think you'll have to do that tonight, Michael,"

"And why is that?" he asked him curiously.

"The boss would like to have a word on you,"

"Are you sure she's not lying?"

"I know when a person lies, Michael,"

"Alright, I'll trust you, Professor Pencil,"

Once he walked towards inside her room and before he could say anything, she told him, "I have a new mission for you, Michael,"

"What kind of mission,"

"The one where you can't possibly fail,"

"What is it?"

"I need you to kidnap a kid for me,"

No words came out of his mouth for a minute until he had the courage to ask her, "Where can I find the kid?"

"The forest,"

"But what about--"

"Your friends." she interrupted.

"How do yo--"

"I may be crazy Michael," she interrupted once more, "but I'm not an idiot… are you up for this mission? After all your life is depending on it,"

Once again, no words came out of his mouth for a minute until he told her, "I'm up for this mission, boss,"

"Good," she told him, "but remember if you fail me, I will have to kill you for reals,"

"Yes, White Magician,"

She grinned while Michael left the room and was about to go to the forest.

V

The Kidnap

Andrew, Sophia, their father, and Slime-Boy were now walking into the forest, trying to find the two people. Andrew was holding Slime-Boy's hand while Sophia and her father were walking together.

"Dad, can I ask you a question?"

'What is it, Sophia?"

"What does Andrew see in that thing?"

"He probably sees something innocent,"

"Why, though?"

"He does look innocent, Sophia,"

"To me, he doesn't,"

"How come?"

"I don't know," she told him, "just look at it, it keeps dripping slime everywhere,"

"I thought you said nothing grosses you out,"

"It's not grossing me out, dad," she told him, "it's just weird that his whole body is made out of that stuff,"

"Maybe he had an accident like Andrew,"

"What do you mean like Andrew?" she asked him curiously.

"What I mean is--"

"Shhh..."

Andrew was shushing them, Sophia, their father, and Slime-Boy all looked confused until they heard something from behind them in the bushes as well. They all turned around and suddenly the man jumped at them and was back in his fiery form.

"You again!?" Sophia asked him curiously.

"I'm not here for you two," he told them, "I'm here for him," He pointed at Slime-Boy, Slime-Boy looked scared and confused, "Give me the kid or I will attack all of you,"

"No way, flames!" cried Andrew.

"So be it then!" he told him. Once he began flying directly at Andrew, Andrew pushed Slime-Boy to the right and was suddenly punched by the flaming man on his chest; pushing him to a tree.

"Andrew!" cried Sophia and his father.

"Alright, you did it now!" cried Sophia, angrily. Sophia was about to approach the man until her father grabbed her hand and told her. "No! Sophia's it's too dangerous,"

"Dad, let go!" she cried to him.

"No!"

"I said let go!" she pulled her hand up as high as she could, and suddenly her father was pushed into a tree, "What just happened?" she thought to herself curiously.

"Help!"

Sophia looked behind and saw the man was grabbing Slime-Boy's right hand. Sophia sighed and thought to herself, "I'm going to regret this," She was now running towards the man and jumped as high as she could. She formed a fist and punched the man as hard as she could. The man spat out his blood, looked angrily at Sophia, and told her, "You punched me for the last time, kid," He let go of Slime-Boy and jumped; he was about to attack Sophia until a splash of water attacked him as quickly as it could. He was pushed into a tree; breaking his right hand. He let out a scream of agony, and once he was done, he looked and saw both The Waterman and Plant-Woman. Sophia and Slime-Boy noticed them as well.

"You again!" he cried to them.

"That's right," said Plant-Woman, "it's time you leave these guys alone,"

"I only want him!" He pointed at Slime-Boy, "and no one else!"

"We don't care who you want," said The Waterman, "we only care about stopping you,"

"Please, don't do this," he told them.

"Why?"

"Because I know who you two are," he told them, "Blue Sky and Green Dirt,"

The two looked shocked at him, Plant-Woman asked him, "How do you…?"

"If you allow me to take the boy," he told them, "I will tell you anything you want once this is all over,"

The two looked at each other for a minute, they looked back at the man and told him, "No,"

"So be it then!" He was back in his fiery form, he flew up in the sky and began firing his fire with his hands while The Waterman began splashing his water at the fire with his hands. Suddenly, the water hit the man and began to almost fall until he decided to turn back into his fiery form and pushed both Blue Sky and Green Dirt into the water. Once they were all in the water, Blue used his powers to form a fist and punch the man as quickly as he could; which made him jump back into the top of the hill. Suddenly, Green rose up by using her plants; it almost looked like a beanstalk. She then used her plants to attack the man, the man tried turning back into his fiery form but was clawed ten times from the plants, he let out another scream of agony while Blue got back up on the hill and punched him directly in the face with his huge fist; he was pushed once more into a tree. He suddenly turned back into his fiery form, grabbed Slime-Boy, and flew as quickly as he could while Slime-Boy let out a scream.

"Oh no…" Sophia thought to herself. She then looked at her father laying all painfully on the ground, and shouted as quickly as she could, "Dad!"

Green returned back to the top of the hill, she noticed Blue was looking at the girl trying to help her father; they both felt bad. Sophia looked at both of them, and then at Andrew who was back up from his healing, and finally at them again, "All of you please help me pick him up! We can't leave him like this!" Andrew approached her and helped Sophia by pulling him up while both Blue and Green decided to help as well by pulling him up too.

"Where should we take him, Andrew?" asked Sophia (who was sobbing), curiously, "A hospital?"

"If we take him to the hospital," he told her, "they'll recognize you,"

"Then where should we take him?"

"We know where," said Blue.

Sophia and Andrew looked at Blue and Green.

Meanwhile back with the bad guys, Professor Pencil heard Michael coming back to the hideout, he gave a sigh and told him, "Let me guess you…" He paused his sentence and saw the slime kid, "actually did it…?"

"Is she still in her room?" he asked him curiously.

"She's always in her room,"

"Good,"

Once he got inside of her room and walked towards her room, he shouted to her, "I have the kid!" He then tossed him on the floor. Slime-Boy looked all scared and confused until he noticed up in the room, a rabbit sitting in a technological, flying chair. She grinned and told Michael, "Good job, Michael. Looks like you get to have a life after all," Slime-Boy was even more horrified and confused.

"Who are you?" Slime-Boy curiously asked her, "And what do you want from me?"

"Hello, Slime-Boy." she told him, "I am The White Magician… I want you because I want answers from you,"

"I'm sorry lady," he told her, frightened, "but I don't have any answers for you,"

She laughed as crazily as she could, "You're funny! But seriously if you don't tell me any answers, I will murder you!" There were no words from Slime-Boy, he was sobbing slowly after he gasped and put his arms into his mouth.

"Aw, does the little green, slimy boy want to cry back to his mama and papa?" she told him, "Well you can't! Because they'll be too disgusted to even see a creature like you!" She laughed once again.

"You're a monster for thinking about that!" he cried to her, angrily.

"Why thank you..." She then muttered words out of her mouth, and suddenly a jar popped out of nowhere on her left hand, "Tell me, boy, do you really not have bones anymore?"

Slime-Boy gave her a confused look.

"If you do, then this will hurt a lot," she told him.

Slime-Boy was confused until he felt something odd inside of his body, he was floating and stretching as fast as he could and landed inside the jar. He gave out a scream of horror while at it. Once she closed the jar, The White Magician laughed as Slime-Boy let out one tear on his right eye.

VI

The Mastermind's Plan

Once Andrew and Sophia's father opened both of his eyes, the only thing he could see was Sophia's green and shiny beautiful face. "Where am I?"

"You're in a big treehouse, dad,"

He was confused until he got a little up and noticed the large house was made entirely out of wood.

"How did I get here?"

"We got you here," said Plant-Woman, who was standing right next to her friend, Waterman.

"And you two are?"

"Plant-Woman,"

"The Waterman,"

"Wait," he said, "you two are the ones who saved my children from that flaming man!"

"Well twice actually," said Plant-Woman.

He was confused and then noticed Andrew in the corner, "Andrew, what's wrong?"

"He got him," he replied in a soft tone.

"What?"

"Who cares really," said Sophia, "you didn't even know him, Andrew,"

Andrew then turned around and shouted to Sophia, "I may not know him, but I wanted to help him!"

"Andrew!" cried his father.

"Oh, so he's more important than your friggin family!" she shouted to him.

"Sophia!" cried her father.

"I'm not saying that!" he shouted to him, "I help people, Sophia! That's what superheroes do unlike you,"

"You think I want to be a superhero?"

"You fell in toxic waste," he told her, "in the comics, every superhero gets his or her powers from an accident,"

"Like you!?"

"With that attitude young lady," he told her, "I think you are going to be the worst superhero ever, Sophia,"

"I don't even have frigging superpowers, Andrew!" She pulled her hand up as high as she could, and suddenly Andrew was pushed through the wooden wall. Everybody saw but thankfully Andrew was alright, however, he had splinters in some parts of his body. Thankfully, he could heal pretty fast. He flew back inside. Once he did, Sophia asked Andrew, "Andrew, are you alright?"

"That's it," he told her.

"What's it?"

"Sophia answer this question as fast as you can," he told her.

"What question?"

"Whenever you pull out your hand," he told her, "does someone get pushed out of nowhere?"

"Come to think of it," she told him, "yeah it has happened,"

"Sophia, you are no longer a normal girl anymore,"

"What are you saying?"

"I'm saying that the toxic waste gave you superpowers,"

"What kind of powers?"

"Telekinesis,"

Sophia and everyone were all shocked at what Andrew just said.

"How do you know it's telekinesis?"

"Whenever you pull out your hand," he told her, "you are pushing the person without even touching them,"

"You're saying that I'm," she told him, "I'm,"

"A superhero,"

"I can't be a superhero!" she cried to Andrew.

"Hey," he told her, "you have to accept it, Sophia… look I know what it feels like, when I had my powers I didn't want to become a superhero too, which is why I became a sidekick. But once my sidekick days were over, I had no choice but to become a superhero. And now it's your turn to become one Radioactive-Girl,"

Sophia was all frightened at what she heard. She turned around and took five steps. She took two deep breaths, looked back at Andrew, and told him, "Don't call me that!"

"Radioactive-Girl?" asked Andrew, curiously.

"Yes!" she told him, "It sounds ridiculous,"

"It sounds heroic Sophia,"

"It's not heroic!" she shouted to him, "It's annoying,"

"Sophia," he told her, "you don't really have a choice but you must become what you were destined to be… in fact," he then looked at both Blue and Green, "You two must also become superheroes,"

They both laughed until they saw Andrew's look of confusion and told him, "You're serious?"

"Blue, you have the powers to control and absorb water…" he told him, he then looked at Green, "and green, you have the power to possibly control and absorb plants,"

"Look Andrew," Blue told him, "just because we saved your guys life, doesn't mean me and Green are superheroes,"

"But it does," he told him, "what you two did was heroic and brave,"

"We don't know," he told him, "what if people fear us?"

"At first they will," he replied, "but they will then look at you as a symbol of heroism, and who knows one day we will never be feared again."

"Even if we are superheroes, Andrew," Sophia told him, "don't we need costumes and capes?"

"Sometimes a superhero doesn't need a costume or a cape," Andrew said.

"Yeah, but I need one if we're going to save Slime-Boy," she told him, "because if I'm really going to become a superhero, my first good act would have to be saving the boy in distress,"

"I agree," he replied to her, "and luckily, we already have fabric,"

He then looked at a bunch of fabric on the right side; Blue and Green have been collecting fabric in order to make clothes, they're really great at it. Blue would always sew the clothes while Green would always cut the fabric.

Andrew looked at both Blue and Green and told them, "Would you two please help us on saving Slime-Boy?"

The two looked at each other, then back at Andrew and told him, "Yes,"

"Great," he told them, "now let's make a costume for Sophia,"

Green was cutting long orange and white fabric, and then Blue was stitching the white with the orange and then making it a suit. Once he was done making the suit, Green had to once again cut the orange fabric, and then Blue stitched it to the back of the suit; making it a cape. Once they were finished, they showed it to Sophia, Sophia told them, "Not bad although if you two are going to make a superhero suit, doesn't it at least need a symbol?" The two looked at the suit, looked at each other, and finally looked back at Sophia and told her, "What kind of symbol?"

"If I'm going to be called Radioactive-Girl," she told them, "I know which symbol I would need in order to make this work,"

Sophia decided to help the two by drawing an image of her symbol and showing it to both Blue and Green. They both agreed and started to work once more with Green cutting a little bit of the white fabric, and Blue stitching the white fabric onto the orange front. Once they were done, they showed it to Sophia, instead of replying back to them, she gave a smile and decided to hug them both while smiling. They hugged her back with a smile.

Once Sophia was done on the ground; putting on her suit, Andrew and the rest were waiting for her.

"Do you really think she's a superhero, Andrew?" his father asked him curiously, "I mean she would be great, but do you really think just because she was in an accident makes her a superhero?"

"Of course," he told him, "you remember when I told you when I had my superpowers,"

"I guess you're right," he replied.

Suddenly, the four heard footsteps climbing up the ladder; it was Sophia. Once Sophia got back up, she asked everyone, "How do I look?" They all looked at her and saw she had a great costume with a mask even covering her identity and a symbol of radiation for her name.

"You look heroic," said Andrew.

"You look beautiful, sweetie," said her father.

"You look great," said Blue.

"You look good," said Green, "although, your feet would hurt since after all it's made out of fabric,"

"I can't be fighting evil if my feet are going to hurt," said Sophia.

"I have an idea," She then went to the right, opened the closet, and grabbed something out of it. She walked back to Sophia with small white boots and told her, "These were once mine when I was your age," she told her, "and now their yours, Sophia"

"No, I shouldn't,"

"No, I insist," she told her, "they'll look great for you,"

"If you say so,"

Sophia grabbed the small white boots and put them on. Once she put them on, everyone looked at her all amazed as if she were a real-life superhero.

"Do I still look heroic Andrew?" Sophia asked him curiously.

"You look even more heroic than you did before,"

"What about you dad," Sophia told him, "do I still look beautiful?"

"You look even more beautiful, Sophia," he told her.

"Thanks, Andrew, thanks dad," she told them with a smile. She looked at Blue and told him, "And what about you Blue, do I still look great?"

"You look greater than you did before, Sophia,"

She chuckled and told him, "Thanks," She then looked at Green and told her, "Thank you,"

"You're welcome," she replied.

"Now, let's save Slime-Boy!" she told them as she put her arms between her body.

"What about me?" asked Andrew and Sophia's father, curiously.

"You have to stay here father," said Andrew.

"Why?" he asked him, "I could fight,"

"No, it's not that," he told him, "Your spine is broken, and you must be able to heal here."

"What if I need some water?" he asked him curiously, "And no, there's no way I'm going to be drinking from Waterman,"

"Don't worry about it Mister Luck," Blue told him, "not even I would think of doing something disgusting like that,"

Andrew then walked towards the right side of the house and grabbed about three stacks of water bottles. He placed it right next to his father, and told him, "If you're ever thirsty, just grab one or two water bottles and drink for once a day because we don't know how long it will take us to save Slime-Boy," His father nodded and smiled back at both him and Sophia, he then told Andrew and Sophia, "Make me proud you two," Andrew and Sophia smiled back at him.

Meanwhile back with the bad guys,

"Do you know who the green girl is?" The White Magician asked Slime-Boy, curiously.

"I don't know anything!" Slime-Boy replied.

Suddenly, Slime-Boy felt pain inside of his body as if something was burning inside of him. It then stopped and he was breathing as heavily as he could in pain.

"I'm going to ask once more," she told him, "either you tell me who she is or I'll burn your insides once more, you little slime!"

"I don't know!" he shouted to her.

The White Magician pulled out her left hand, and suddenly Slime-Boy let out a scream of agony once more. She formed her hand as a fist, and Slime-Boy screamed so loud that it shattered a little piece of the glass. She gasped and stopped. Slime-Boy was sweating slime while shedding some tears.

"Aw, does the little green baby want to be breastfed by his own mama?"

"You're a monster!" he still shed some tears.

"A monster?" she told him, "Once again, thank you for your kind words, little green boy,"

Slime-Boy kept on weeping some tears while The White Magician felt annoyed. She looked back at Slime-Boy and told him, "Either you tell me who she is or I'll burn your green, slimy insides you little slime ball,"

"What if I break the glass with my scream?"

She quickly snapped her fingers, and suddenly the crack was no longer there. Slime-Boy looked all worried and horrified.

"You can scream all you want boy," she told him, "but it ain't going to break this glass prison,"

"Freak!" he cried to her, angrily.

"Once again, thank you,"

"Even if I did know," he told her, "why would I tell you?"

The White Magician suddenly laughed as crazily as she could. Slime-Boy looked all concerned and still horrified.

"Why are you laughing...?" he asked her curiously, "You think this is some kind of joke you crazy witch!"

She stopped laughing, looked directly at Slime-Boy, and told him, "Because if you don't want me to screw your life, and if you want your precious family to be safe, so you better tell me boy, who is she!?"

"You don't even know who I am!" he cried to her, angrily.

"Oh, but I will," She laughed as crazily as she could while Slime-Boy still looked concerned and horrified.

Meanwhile back with the good guys, the four were beginning to walk outside of the forest and Sophia asked Andrew a question, "Why can't you just fly us?"

"Because I saw something below here,"

"What did you see?" she asked him curiously.

"You'll see,"

Once the four were outside of the forest, both Andrew and Sophia walked outside while Blue and Green looked concerned. Andrew noticed and asked, "What's wrong?"

"We've been outside the forest before," said Blue, "it's just I feel like this will be the last time we'll go back to the forest ever again,"

"Why would you ask such a question?"

"Because my gut gas a feeling, Andrew,"

"Look, trust me," he told them, "nothing bad will happen to the both of you,"

"You promise?" Green asked him curiously.

"I swear to myself,"

Blue and Green looked at each other, then back at Andrew, and both stepped outside of the forest. After a minute had passed, Sophia stepped on something squishy, she looked down at her shoe and it was green slime!

"Guys, I found something!" she cried to them.

Andrew, Blue, and Green looked at her and noticed the green slime on the bottom of her right boot. Andrew approached Sophia and told her, "Sophia, don't move," Andrew grabbed some of the slime and examined it, he then looked down and saw a trail of green slime. Sophia noticed it, and Blue and Green noticed it as well. They all smiled.

"Everyone follow me," he told them.

Meanwhile back with the bad guys, Michael was walking towards Professor Pencil and told him, "Professor may I ask you a question?"

"Of course, Michael,"

"When did you meet her?"

"The White Magician?"

"Yes, her,"

"It's a long story,"

"I have time to hear it,"

"Very well," he told him, "it all began last year in December, I was doing my average day in my mother's house. Once I finished reading The Adventures of Pinocchio, which is very different from Disney's adaptation, the doorbell rang. I wondered if it was my poor, sick mother, so I decided to answer the door. Before I could do that, I had to see through the peephole, and I saw a big girl in a magician's outfit. She was looking down. I asked who she was, and she replied with, "I want to talk to you." I was at first confused about what she meant by that, so I asked her once again, "Who is this?" She replied once more, "I just want to talk to you," I told her she was in the wrong house until she told me, "I know who you are, Professor Pencil," I was first in shock, so I told her once more, "Who is this?" she replied saying, "It's alright, I'm not here to hurt you, I'm here to help you," I didn't want to open the door until I decided to be a man and opened the door, and there I saw her, The White Magician. I was amazed

I wasn't the only one who was born differently, I knew because of the way she looks. Once I opened the door, she looked up and gave me a grin, an uncomfortable grin. I wanted to close the door but I was too scared until she told me, "Before you dare close the door, may I at least come in?" I then let her in, we both talked in the living room, I asked her what she wanted, and she replied with, "I want to help you make your machine," I was again shocked and played dumb with her, "What machine?" She laughed crazily and I was confused as to why until she looked at me and told me, "I'm not an idiot, Professor Pencil! I know you're building a machine to turn everyone like you, and I want to help you," I was at first silent, and asked her, "Why?" she replied with, "I believe people are getting more and more stupid every day from not skipping school to making silly YouTube videos on their phones," I replied with, "What do you want?" she replied to me saying, "A chance for us to change the world Pencil," I told her, "What can you do?" she replied with, "I have the parts you need in order to complete your machine," I thought about it for five seconds until I asked her, "What's the catch?" She replied with, "No catch, just a machine," After many minutes of thinking, I smiled and agreed with her, she then pulled out her left hand and told me, "Let's shake on it," I shook her hand, and the rest is history, my friend,"

"What about your mother?" he asked him curiously.

"As for my poor mother," he told him, "I had to get her permission as well, however, and sadly, my poor mother hanged herself on a bridge. I had to leave the house and live here after that,"

"I'm so sorry for that, Professor Pencil," Michael said.

"It's alright Michael," he replied to him, "it's all part of God's plan after all,"

Meanwhile back with the good guys, the four stepped outside a clothing store and the trail of slime was leading them into a manhole.

"Why would somebody with fire powers go down a sewer?" Blue asked curiously.

"I don't know Blue," he told him, "but we're going to find out," He grabbed the manhole and placed it down as softly as he could, "You go first Blue,"

Blue went down the manhole, Green went down as well, Sophia then looked at Andrew and told him, "It's a good thing, I've smelled worse,"

He chuckled, patting her on the head with his right brown, wing, and told her, "Me too," Sophia then climbed down the ladder, Andrew did the same, however, he grabbed the manhole cover and placed it back where it was once he climbed down the smelly sewers. They were now walking towards the slime trail. Once ten minutes had passed, Andrew finally had to ask both Blue and Green while walking, "Do you know him?"

"Hmmm...?"

"The fireman?" he asked them, "Do you know who he is?"

"No," they both replied to him.

"But he does look a bit familiar," said Green.

"What do you mean, Green?" Blue asked her curiously.

"I mean, for starters, how did he know our names?"

"Come to think of it, you're right," he replied to her, "he does look a bit familiar and how did he know our names too?"

"Was he an old friend of yours?" Andrew asked them curiously.

"Why would you ask that, Andrew?" Blue asked him curiously.

"Just wondering," he replied.

"All we could tell you is we don't know," replied Blue.

"Alright,"

Thirty minutes had passed, and the slime trail was now leading them to a door. Sophia tried opening it with her right hand. She then told the others, "It's locked,"

"Step aside, Sophia," said Andrew.

Sophia was walking backward to the right side, Andrew then formed a fist on his right feather and punched the door as hard as he could. They all looked at the inside and noticed it was all dark but could see a lot of slime.

"Come on," Andrew told them.

Once the four stepped inside the room, they could now see a lot of light thanks to Sophia's green glowing body.

"If we see a killer clown with a red balloon here," Sophia told them, "I'm going to punch it in its stupid frigging face,"

"Really?" Andrew asked her curiously.

"Hey," she told him, "just saying, Andrew,"

Once twenty minutes had passed, they could see another door, Sophia tried opening it with her right hand, she gave a heavy sigh and thought to herself, "Not again,"

"Alright Andrew," she told him, "do your thing,"

Andrew then punched the door open, they could once again see darkness in the other room.

"Sophia lead us the way," Andrew told her.

Once the four stepped inside the room, they could still see the trail of slime, however, once they followed it, it led to another door, but this time it was two enormous doors.

"This looks like something out of Andrew's silly comic books or a cartoon," Sophia thought to herself.

"How are we going to open that door?" Blue asked them curiously.

"In comics," said Andrew, "you just push it as hard as you can,"

"Go ahead Andrew," Sophia told him, "push it, after all, you are the comic book nerd,"

Once Andrew pushed the doors, they could see half of the slime trail and a desk. On top of it was Slime-Boy trapped in a jar! Slime-Boy noticed them and was making a worried look.

"It's Slime-Boy!" Sophia cried to them, "Come on!"

Sophia ran as fast as she could inside the room, Andrew cried to her, "Sophia, wait!" Once Sophia grabbed the jar, she could see Slime-Boy crying.

"Are you crying?"

Suddenly, Slime-Boy gasped and told her, "It's a trap!" Suddenly, Andrew, Blue, and Green were pushed by the man in orange clothing and a talking pencil. Once Sophia looked, she thought to herself, "Is that a talking pencil...? This night couldn't get any weirder,"

"Oh but it can,"

She looked up and saw a large, talking rabbit dressed up in a magician's outfit (who was sitting in a floating chair) with a grin on her face.

"And, I stand corrected," she said.

"You must be the girl," the rabbit said, "nice to meet finally meet you,"

"Who are you supposed to be?" she asked the rabbit curiously, "The White Rabbit combined with The Mad Hatter?"

"Oh, I think you know exactly who I am," she grinned.

Once Sophia looked into her eyes, she gave a gasp and thought to herself, "It can't be,"

"That's right!" she told her, "I'm The White Magician!"

"To be honest," she told her, "I thought you would at least look more human,"

"I get that a lot," she laughed as crazily as she could.

"What is she laughing at?" she thought to herself curiously.

"No reason!" she told her.

Sophia looked all horrified and disturbed by what she heard.

"Aw, does the little green shiny girl want to hug her big brother because she's scared?"

"Leave my sister alone, you witch!"

She gave out an angry look, looked back at him, and told him while she once again grinned, "Bird! It's good to see my favorite sparrow once more again," She pulled out her large tongue and licked out her dry lips.

"Good to see you too, White Magician," he replied, angrily.

"Got to be honest my sparrow," she told him, "it hasn't been the same without fighting you, honestly, it hasn't,"

"Good to know that, you sick rabbit," he told her, angrily.

"Aw, Bird," she told him in a depressed-like look, "you're hurting my own feelings, boohoo," she laughed as crazily as she could.

"You're sick," he told her, "you know that,"

Once she stopped laughing, she told him, "Oh, I know Bird, and boy, do I love it!" She then looked at a man whose body was made out of the water and a woman whose body was made out of plants, she then looked back at Bird and told him, "New friends of yours, sparrow?" Blue and Green noticed the rabbit and both gave out a horrified look at it.

"What on mother nature's earth is that?" Green asked.

"I'm a rabbit, as you can see," she replied, "and you're a very stupid plant," She once laughed as crazily as ever.

"Hey!" cried Green, angrily.

"Don't yell at Green like that, you demon!" shouted Blue, angrily.

"Finally!" cried The White Magician, "Somebody who calls me what I actually am,"

"Crazy," Blue thought to himself.

"Why thank you," she replied.

"What the...?"

"She can read minds, Blue," Andrew said.

"Aw Bird," The White Magician told him, "why are you always spoiling the fun whenever you're around?"

"Look creep, you better leave us alone!" cried Sophia, annoyed, "Or I'll, I'll,"

"I'll, I'll!" she mocked her, "You'll what kid? Bore me!? Hahahahaha!"

Sophia gave out an angry look, she pulled her arm as high as she could and tried pushing The White Magician but was too late since she was pushed mentally by The White Magician herself. She bumped into Bird, and the three fell down onto the floor. Blue and Green helped them get back up while The White Magician laughed as crazily as she could, "Aw, does the baby sister want to hug her big baby brother, along with her green boyfriend?"

"Boyfriend!?" she cried to her, angrily, "You just messed with the wrong girl, rabbit!"

She ran and jumped as high as she could, "Now face my knuckle sandwich!" Suddenly, the rabbit punched her on the right top of her face with her hard right fist and on the left bottom on her face with her hard left fist. Sophia fell down onto The White Magician's desk and onto the floor. She spat a tooth out and both her and Andrew gasped while The White Magician laughed as crazily as she could, "You're an adorable little green girl!" she still laughed while Sophia began weeping her tears.

"Aw, does the little green girl want to cry back to his mommy and daddy?" She laughed once more as crazily as she could.

Andrew noticed, he formed a fist on his right hand, and gave out a scream of anger, "Hey you witch!" The White Magician suddenly stopped laughing, looked at Bird with an angry look while he told her, "You want to fight someone? Fight me!" He flew up and was about to punch her in the face while screaming until she told him, "With pleasure my little sparrow," She licked her own lips once more, she then jumped at Bird while giving a scream to him, and the two landed down onto the ground; breaking his back for a little (he let out a small scream of agony) until his back healed again. The White Magician clawed him on the chest.

"Andrew!" Sophia cried to him, worried.

Bird punched The White Magician on the face and was about to jump at her until he stopped moving above the air, The White Magician then jumped at him while screaming, she pushed him into a wall (which led back to the sewers) and began drowning his head in the disgusting water. However, fortunately, he had the strength to put his head back up and spat all the sewer water at The White Magician's face. Once she opened her eyes again, she was once again punched in the face by Bird. She was pushed to a wall, and right where Bird was going to punch her back, she turned invisible. Bird only hit the wall. He stood up and was curious about where she was until he was punched twice by her and moved as well. He was pushed into the right wall and into the left wall about three times. He could hear her sinister laugh. He then spat directly at her.

"Really again!?" The White Magician cried to herself. Once she was visible and opened her eyes, she was once again punched by him. She spat out a tooth, Bird was about to punch her until she caught her punch, looked at him with an angry look, and twisted his right-wing. The Bird let out a scream of agony. She punched him in the right side of his ribs as hard as she could, he spat out his own blood. She pulled her leg up and twisted his leg. He once again let out a scream of agony. She then hugged him and pulled him up as high as she could with all of her strength and began crushing him. He began groaning.

"How does it feel, my little sparrow?" The White Magician told him, "Oh, please say at least one thing to me or I'll have to give you a big kiss on your black and pointy beak," She pulled out her large tongue and began licking his black and pointy beak as slowly as she could. She then pushed out her hands as tightly as she could, he once again let out a scream of agony. Suddenly, he could hear his spine crack from his insides. He let out a small breath and his eyes were as big as ever. The White Magician dropped him onto the disgusting floor, "Oops, maybe I might have broken your spine, my cute sparrow..." she let out a huge sinister laugh to herself, "it's a good thing you can heal, but for now, you're coming with me," She patted him on his featherhead, picked him up by his head with her left hand and began walking towards her room.

"Andrew?" asked Sophia, curiously and concerned.

Once The White Magician stepped inside her room, Sophia noticed Andrew beneath her left hand, he was bleeding from his mouth. Sophia yelled out his name, "Andrew!"

"It's alright little green girl," She then threw him down as hard as she could in the middle of the room, "his spine's only broken from his insides, and what's the matter anyway, he can heal, can't he?" she laughed as crazily as she could.

Sophia gave out an angry look. Suddenly, Sophia could move again (the rest of them were being controlled by her) and she formed a fist on her right hand, she got back up and ran towards The White Magician while shouting to her, "I'll kill ya, you evil witch!" The White Magician stopped laughing, looked back at Sophia all angry and insane. Once Sophia was about to jump at her with her fist, she pulled out her hand and mentally pushed Sophia into a wall; hurting her back. She landed down on the floor and slept. The White Magician laughed as crazily as ever while Slime-Boy kept crying.

Once she woke up from her sleep, she noticed she was in a dark unknown room. Thankfully her body was glowing like a lantern. She noticed Blue and Green, however, they were trapped in jars as well. She wanted to get to them but her hands were chained up to the wall. Sophia then remembered her brother saying she had telekinesis, she tried using it as hard as she could. However, sadly, nothing happened. She let out a heavy sigh and looked down at the messy floor.

"Hi,"

She looked to her right and saw Slime-Boy (who was still trapped inside of a jar and stopped crying) giving a smile to her. She gave him an angry look, so mad that she didn't even want to talk to him and look away from him. Once a minute had passed, Slime-Boy asked her curiously, "Did I do something wrong?"

"Oh, you did Slime-Boy," she told him.

"What did I do?"

"I'll tell you exactly what you did, Slime-Boy..." she then turned her head back towards him and shouted to him, "you're the reason why my brother got injured by a frigging rabbit! And you're also the reason why me, Blue, and Green are in this mess!"

"I'm sorry," he replied, "I didn't mean to,"

She chuckled, "You didn't mean to, of course, you didn't mean to," She then told him while looking at him eye to eye, "Well guess what, I don't give a darn about it you stupid Slime-Boy!"

"Look," he told her, "I tried warning you,"

"Oh and thank you for that," she replied.

"She was controlling my mouth!" he yelled.

"She was controlling all of us, you idiot!" she yelled.

"Look, I didn't mean to be turned into this thing,"

"And I didn't mean to put on this ridiculous costume," she told him, "in order to save your frigging life, you stupid slime ball!"

They stopped looking at each other and were both silent for twelve minutes until Slime-Boy cried as slowly as he could.

"Not again with the crying," Sophia thought to herself.

She looked back at him and asked him curiously, "What are you even crying about?"

"I'm crying because I'll never confess my love to her,"

"I'm sorry?" she asked him curiously.

"I'll never confess my love to this cute, tall girl,"

"Cute tall girl?" she thought to herself curiously. She then looked back at him and asked him curiously, "What age is she?"

"What do you care,"

"Please,"

"She's probably in the same age as me," he told her, "12,"

"What's the color of her hair?"

"Orange like yours but not glowing,"

"And the color of her eyes?"

"Come to think of it, they're also orange like... yours...?" he then looked back at her while she gave him a look.

Sophia then asked him curiously, "What school do you go to...?"

"Forest Middle," he replied to her, "I was in a summer school field trip,"

"Me too," she told him.

They looked at each other for about four minutes until Slime-Boy told her, "You're he aren't you, you're Sophia Smith,"

"How do you know my name?"

"We go to the same P.E. class,"

"Oh yeah," she replied, she then gave a look as well as blushing, "Oh my god,"

"What?"

"I am so sorry!" she cried to him.

"Sorry for what?"

"For calling you a freak of nature and more,"

"Why are you apologizing too?"

"Because.." she told him, "because... because you seemed like a nice kid when I saw you back in my school,"

"Thanks," he told her, "since when?"

"Since the beginning of my first year," she told him, "What's your name?"

"My name...?" he asked her curiously, "Don't you already know it?"

"I don't listen to the teacher when she calls everyone's names,"

He laughed until he noticed a look on Sophia's face, "Oh, you're serious, sorry,"

"That's alright Slime-Boy," he replied.

He chuckled and told her, "Thanks Sophia, but my name is actually--" Suddenly, the door opened. The two wondered who it was until the man in orange stepped inside the room in his fiery form.

"You!" Sophia cried to him.

"Shhhhh...."

"No, I have some words for you mister!" he told her, "For starters, I'm going to kick your as--"

The man then covered up Sophia's mouth with his right hand and once again shushed at her. She still looked very angry until he whispered to her right ear, "I want to help you," Sophia looked all confused and curious, he then melted the chains, Sophia easily broke free, stood up, picked, and smashed the glass jar once she picked it up. Slime-Boy was finally free! Slime-Boy then looked at Sophia and gave her a big hug and told her, "Thank you!" She was blushing once more until the man told them, "Can you two please stop and help me free your friends," Sophia and Slime-Boy each grabbed a jar and broke it, freeing both Blue and Green. Once they gasped, Blue asked, "What the heck happened...?" he and Green then looked at the man and told him, "You!?" Blue and Green stood up and were about to attack the man until Sophia stopped them and told them, "It's alright, he's here to free us!"

The two looked concerned at Sophia until the man told the two, "Just follow me, and I'll tell you everything!" Once they all stepped outside the room, they were now running towards the sewers.

"Who are you and how do you know our names?" Blue asked him curiously.

"My name is Michael E," he said, "I know you because we used to know each other, Blue and Green,"

Blue and Green stopped, and Green asked Michael curiously, "What do you mean we used to know each other?"

"We have a history together," he told them, "you just forgot about it,"

"We would like to ask more questions, Michael," she told him, "but I think it's best if we save Andrew first along with telling us what the heck is going on,"

"Of course,"

The four were running as fast as they could while Michael told them, "The White Magician doesn't want to really help Professor Pencil,"

"Wait, I'm sorry, Professor Pencil...?" Sophia asked him curiously.

"Yes, that's his name."

"Real or supervillain name?"

"He's not the one you should be worried about," he told her, "neither should I."

"What a weird name," Sophia thought to herself. She then told him, "You were attacking us,"

He gave a sigh and told her, "Because she told me to,"

"What do you mean?"

"Ever since I gave her some radiation," he told her, "she told me to get you in the forest,"

"How does she know where I was?"

"If I tell you," he told her, "you'll freak out about it,"

"You attacked us because a rabbit told you too,"

"Exactly,"

"What about Slime-Boy?"

"She told me to kidnap him,"

"I really hate this rabbit boss of yours," she replied to him.

"Me too," said Slime-Boy.

Sophia looked at him while blushing, she then looked back at Michael and told him, "If you hate her, why are you working for her?"

"It's complicated," he replied to her.

"Michael," Green said, "what did you mean about her not helping Professor Pencil?"

"I mean she's not building a machine to turn everyone smarter," he told them, "She's tricking him into building a machine to kill everyone including herself,"

The three stopped and told him, "What!?" Once Michael stopped as well, he gave a heavy sigh, looked back, and told them, "I know, it sounds crazy," he told them, "but so is she,"

"Why on earth would she want to do that?" Sophia asked him curiously.

"No reason,"

"But every supervillain has to have a reason," said Slime-Boy.

"Every but White Magician," said Sophia.

"How is she even going to do it?" Green asked him curiously.

"We must first go back in the room,"

"No, you better tell us right now," she told him, "we deserved to know the truth,"

He sighed and told them, "You want the truth, fine... Ever since she became crazy, The White Magician has been thinking of a plan to kill everyone, even her loved ones. Suddenly, one day, the idea came to her, building a machine unleashing a large beam of power that could wipe out all of Humankind, Gifts, and even nature. For Humankind and Gifts, their brains would become larger and explode. As for nature, it would kill them slowly in their insides. There would be nothing left of the planet but death, and I need your help to stop her before she kills all of us and before it's too late."

The three looked concerned and shocked at each other.

"That's a messed up rabbit," said Sophia.

"Michael, why does The White Magician need Professor Pencil's help?"

"She needed a scientist to build the machine,"

"Why can't she do it?"

"If she did it," he told them, "then we'll all be dead because she hates being patient,"

"What exactly are we below right now?" Slime-Boy asked him.

"The Land of Magnificent,"

'The theme park...?" Sophia asked him curiously, "Wait a minute, how long have we been asleep?"

"For many hours," Michael replied to her.

"Is it daytime or a new nighttime?"

"A new nighttime,"

"What's today?"

"The 27th,"

"Oh no," said Sophia.

"What's wrong?" Slime-Boy asked her curiously.

"Tonight's the 50th anniversary," she told him, "Micahel, how does the machine work?"

"Professor Pencil just has to put his head into the machine, and it'll activate itself immediately."

"She's going to trick Professor Pencil into using his mind to murder all of us at the park's 50th anniversary,"

"If she does that," Slime-Boy told her, "then no more humans and nature,"

"We have to stop her then!" Green cried to them, "Or she'll kill all of us!"

After walking for many minutes, the four were back in The White Magician's room where they could see Andrew still asleep and locked up inside a birdcage.

"Andrew!" Sophia cried to him worryingly. Sophia pulled out her right hand as fast as she could and tried moving the huge birdcage, however, Michael told her to stop as well as telling her, "If you want your brother to be set free, we must stop The White Magician first,"

"Alright," she muttered to him.

"Everyone search around," Michael told them.

Sophia was checking inside her closet with Slime-Boy; all they could find were newspapers of her fighting Andrew as Bird as well as a shrine to Bird himself. The two were concerned about what they were seeing.

"So your brother's Bird?" Slime-Boy asked her curiously.

"Yeah,"

"That's actually cool," he told her, "but you're cool too, it's just I'm a big fan of his."

"It's alright,"

"Is it me or is this White Magician a complete weirdo around your brother?"

Sophia then looked back at Slime-Boy and told him, "What was your first clue, Slime-Boy?" They both laughed with each other while Blue and Green were looking behind the desk; nothing.

"So do you really think we could become superheroes, Green?" Blue asked her curiously.

"If we save a bunch of people," Green told him, "but promise me I wouldn't have to wear such a ridiculous outfit,"

He chuckled and told her, "I'm pretty sure you won't,"

"Thanks, Blue,"

Michael was looking above the desk, and suddenly he found a remote he clicked on it, and it activated all the televisions. They were the cameras, however, he saw one connected to the sewers, he decided to replay it, and once he did, he gave out a look of surprise, dropped the remote, and told everyone, "We need to leave, right now!"

"Why?" they asked him curiously until they heard a familiar sinister laugh from above. Suddenly, the chair turned around and something visible appeared, it was The White Magician! She then pulled out her hands and controlled everyone in the room but her and Professor Pencil who was still asleep outside of her room.

"Hello again!" she told the good guys, "It's so good to see you alright except for you," She then gave an angry look and turned to face Michael, who was beneath her. She moved everyone in the middle (they could now talk), however, only Michael was the one standing up on White Magician's control while the rest were kneeling. Professor Pencil was behind them.

"So you think you could betray me?" The White Magician told Michael, "Huh? Well, you were mistaken to even think of such an idiotic idea like that!" She pointed at him, "And now, it's time for you to die," She magically cut off Blue's hand and dumped the water on Michael, and she stopped controlling him by using her hands. Once he began to breathe, The White Magician quickly hugged him as hard as she could. She pushed her hands as tightly as she could, and Michael let out a scream of agony.

"All your bones breaking just makes me gosh darn happy!" she told him, "Wouldn't you agree, Michael?" He began breathing painfully.

"Stop it please!" Slime-Boy cried to her.

She pushed it more hard as she could, Michael let out another scream of agony, "What was that green boy? I couldn't hear you over me crushing this idiot!" Blue and Green were horrified to look at it while Professor Pencil turned his head behind, and was going to look back once it was all over. Sophia was just worried since Michael couldn't heal himself like her brother. The White Magician grinned at Michael's pain. Suddenly, she snapped his entire back, he coughed out blood.

"Mmmmm…" said The White Magician to herself, "I can't wait to lick your blood off my hat, then I'm going to do all those things I mentioned to you… goodbye Michael, tell Jesus I said hello,"

Once she pushed as hard as she could, Michael was gone. She dropped him as hard as she could, and told them, "Now, who's next once I cut off his head?"

Slime-Boy let out bits of tears, Blue and Green let out a tear on their right eye, and Sophia gave a gasp of horror and began sobbing. Professor Pencil looked back and saw Michael's dead, bloody body laying down in the room.

"Oh my…" Professor Pencil thought to himself, horrified.

She then picked up Michael, pulled out her left claw, and cut off his entire head! There was a pool of blood on the floor. All but The White Magician watched in horror.

"You're a monster!" cried Slime-Boy.

"Why thank you, Slime-Boy," she told him with a grin while Slime-Boy looked worried and confused, "I know what you're all thinking, how do I know his name…? Well, I've been watching you with my cameras, and I know who all you people are… that's right Sophia Smith, I know who you are and that your brother is Andrew Luck,"

Sophia gasped.

"I love gasps," she told her, "I also know who you are Blue and Green, and fun fact Micahel used to know who you two were and what your origin was, however, and sadly, you'll probably never get to know that."

"You devil!" Green cried to her, "You killed him! You killed him!"

"Once again, thank you," she then told them, "I also knew all your plans, I had cameras everywhere… I knew you would follow the slime trail, and it will lead you to where I am. I also knew Michael freed all of you because I had cameras all over!"

"Wait if you knew who Sophia was," Slime-Boy told her, "then why would you ask and torture me?"

"For fun!" she laughed as crazily as ever.

"You're a sick girl!"

"Aw, why thank you," she replied, and still laughed as crazily as ever, "and Sophia, do you really think your father is going to be all right in the forest?"

"If you mention my father one more time," she told her, "I will kill you,"

"Threatening me and almost not scared of me," she told her, "I like it, which is why I think you should go next," She pulled out her left hand and stopped controlling Sophia. She fell to the floor and breathed until she stood up and was about to punch The White Magician in the face until she The White Magician stopped controlling the rest of the good guys, they're too weak to get back up and decided to grab Sophia by her shirt and hug her as fast as she could. She began pushing her claws as fast as she could. Sophia groaned. Once she opened her eyes, she looked down at The White Magician and told her, "You demonic--" Before she could finish her sentence, The White Magician pushed her claws even more hard, and Sophia let out a scream of agony.

"I love bearhugs, don't you?" The White Magician told her, "Just because you're adopted doesn't mean you're still not her sibling, and since you're his sibling, he would always give you big hugs as well as once kiss you on your forehead. Oh, how I would love to feel his normal lips, but I can if you let me lick you in your forehead,"

"Never!"

With no words to say to her, The White Magician pulled out her large tongue and began licking Sophia's forehead. Sophia gasped and wanted to get out of her arms, but The White Magician was too strong. Suddenly, she could hear and feel her bones almost breaking from the inside, and was breathing painfully while The White Magician grinned. Slime-Boy noticed, he looked angry, he stretched his head and decided to bite White Magician's left leg. The White Magician screamed, looked down, and noticed his head, so did Sophia. She pulled her left leg as high as she could and stepped on Slime-Boy's face; he felt pain. She then pulled out her left hand and metally controlled Slime-Boy, he was now high up in the air, and she told him, "It's time I burn that body of yours, little green boy!" She then muttered some words out of her mouth, and Slime-Boy was feeling the flames inside of his slimy body, he let out a scream of agony. Once

Sophia heard it, she gasped, looked angry, and told The White Magician, "You demonic WITCH!" Once she bites The White Magician's nose, The White Magician groaned while her blood was spilling out. Sophia easily pulled out her right hand, let out a scream of anger and pushed The White Magician into the wall with her telekinesis. Both her and Slime-Boy fell down the floor hardly while The White Magician was now down outside of her room and inside the sewers, all she did was grinned and laughed a little crazy. Sophia slowly got up from all the pain, looked at Slime-Boy, ran to him, and asked him, "Are you alright?"

"Thank you," he told her in a soft tone, "you're my hero, Sophia Smith,"

Sophia began to blush, "Why no problem, I mean… Andrew!" She looked up, pulled out her hand, and tried breaking the birdcage, however, and sadly, she couldn't.

"Come on!" she thought to herself.

"How adorable!"

Sophia and Slime-Boy both turned to the left and looked at The White Magician, who was back up and stepping inside her room, "I just love it! You use your telekinesis because you don't want your precious love to be hurt by me, oh GOD I just love it!"

"Well, you're going to love this, witch!" Sophia pulled out her right hand and tried moving her, but sadly it wasn't working. The White Magician then pulled out her left hand and was now controlling Sophia, she was up in the air, she could feel her insides getting crushed, "You know I'm beginning to actually hate you, 'Radioactive-Girl'," she told her, "and now it's time for you to die!" Sophia groaned.

"Sophia!" cried Slime-Boy, worryingly

Suddenly, she was splashed in water by Blue and then punched by Green's large, plant fist. She fell down hard, and so did Sophia. She looked at Blue and Green, who were back up.

"I don't think so, you witch!" Blue cried to her.

"Oh, great you two," The White Magician told them. She looked at Professor Pencil and told him, "Why are you just standing there!? Do something!"

"I sadly can't fight," Professor Pencil told her.

"Then you're useless for now!" She pulled out her left hand and pushed Professor Pencil outside her room.

"I guess I'll have to do everything myself!" She then pulled out both of her hands and was controlling both Green and Blue, she was destroying their insides. The two were groaning until she was air-punched by Sophia. She spat out one of her sharp teeth, gasped, looked at Sophia (with Slime-Boy all standing up), and yelled to her angrily, "You've done it now, witch!" She pulled out her claws and was beginning to attack both her and Slime-Boy. Sophia and Slime-Boy tried avoiding the claws, however, and sadly, they got sliced twice. Sophia let out a scream of agony, and so did Slime-Boy.

"I thought you couldn't feel?" Sophia asked him curiously.

"I can't," he told her, "but whenever she hits me, I can actually feel it,"

"It's called magic you little green idiot!" The White Magician cried to him and clawed both Sophia and Slime-Boy on their right cheeks. She then punched both of them. The two were about to punch her back once she jumped, however, she was no longer there and the two were then jumped by her, who clawed them both on their back. The two screamed and fell to the floor. They both groaned. The White Magician grabbed Sophia's head by her hair and pulled out her left claw and told her, "It's time for your head to be cut off!"

Suddenly, she was super punched by Green's large plant fist once again. She spat out another tooth and told herself, "Really! Again!?" She then looked at both Blue and Green. Green told her, "Pick on someone older than you, witch"

"With pleasure, green lady!" She then jumped at both of them while screaming in rage; she was about to attack them until Water Man punched her in the face. Once The White Magician was up in the air, Plant-Woman grabbed her with her branches and threw her down as hard as she could onto her floating chair to her desk, "You can throw me anywhere but at my chair and desk is where I cross the line!" The two then approached what remained of both the chair and desk, however, they didn't see her. Suddenly, Plant-Woman was up in the air and pushed into a wall while Water Man was punched in the face and pushed hard into a wall. The White Magician turned back to visible after she paused time twice.

"Who's next!?" The White Magician yelled out in rage.

"How about me?"

She knew that voice, The White Magician gave a confused look, turned around, and was punched in the face by Bird! She fell down onto the remains of her desk and chair, she looked back up to him and asked curiously, "How?"

"While you were fighting Blue and Green," he told her, "Slime-Boy stretched his body to free me, and once he accidentally dropped me, Sophia woke me up by hitting my back as hard as she could, which got me back healed easily and faster. Sophia also told me what you've been planing, which is why you're under arrest,"

She looked down, and suddenly her eyes were bigger. Once she looked back at him, she began breathing loudly and gave out an angry look, and shouted back to him, "I'll kill you, you little sparrow!" She used one of her arms to push herself, and once she was back up, she hugged Bird (he groaned) and she pushed him up the messy ceiling.

The Land of Magnificent

Once they landed on the ground, The White Magician stood up and saw many people seeing her as a freak of nature while Bird looked up and noticed the people as well.

"It's them!" a man cried, "It's The Bird and The White Magician! They're real!"

Many people gasped while the children were amazed to see The Bird while horrified to see The White Magician. The White Magician let out a growl with her claws up; some people screamed while some gasped including the children.

"Are you getting any of this?" the anchorwoman asked her cameraman curiously to which he nodded.

"Freeze you freaks!" a cop cried out while pulling out his gun.

The White Magician pulled out her left hand and pushed the police officer on the top of a roller coaster ride, which he was crushed by the coaster; people screamed in horror.

"NO!" Bird cried out loud.

"YES, BIRD!" The White Magician cried to him, "You wanted to reveal yourself to the public, well here you go!"

The Bird stood up while people still gasped. He looked at The White Magician with an angry look and told her, "It's time we end this once and for all you crazy rabbit,"

"With pleasure my little sparrow!" She jumped at him and began attacking him by clawing at him while people ran as fast as they could screaming in horror; not wanting to be attacked by her as well.

Bird and The White Magician were clawing the heck out of each other left to right. The White Magician with her hands while Bird with his feet. Bird could heal but not The White Magician. They both let out screams of agony whenever they clawed at each other. The Bird was about to punch her in the face after jumping until he was controlled by her.

"Now what to do with you?" she told herself as she was thinking, she then looked at a huge abandoned roller coaster called "Wonderland", she grinned and told Bird, "It's time for a huge ride my wooden sparrow!" She pushed him on top of the roller coaster ride. He groaned, and once he woke up, The White Magician was about to crush him with her feet until Bird avoided it, and stood back up again.

"Remember when we used to go to roller coasters in our old days?"

"How could I forget old friend,"

"Let's finish this and see who really is the strongest!" she replied.

"With pleasure," He then formed his feathers into a fist, ran towards The White Magician while trying to punch her in the face, however, she kept avoiding them. She then grabbed one of Andrew's feathers and twisted it as hard as she could; Andrew let out a huge scream of agony.

"My turn," she told him. She opened her claws and began clawing Bird in his face, she then formed a fist on her left hand and punched Bird in the face, he fell down onto the floor. He groaned. He quickly got back up and told her angrily, "I'm not done with you yet, you devil!" She screamed and began walking towards him with his claws while Andrew jumped and formed a fist on his right feather.

Meanwhile back in The White Magician's room, Sophia woke up and noticed a hole in the ceiling as well as hearing many people screaming over their lives.

"Oh no," she said.

"What's going on?" Slime-Boy asked her curiously.

"My brother is fighting that crazy witch all by herself up there!" She pointed up to which Slime-Boy noticed, he then told her, "He's going to get himself killed," She gave him a look and Slime-Boy told him, "Sorry," They both then saw Blue and Green groaning.

"Blue!" Sophia cried at them, "Green!"

'We need to help them!" cried Slime-Boy.

Sophia and Slime-Boy stood back up, ran towards Blue and Green, and helped them get back up.

"What happened?" they both asked them curiously.

"That crazy witch is kicking her brother's butt up there!" He pointed up at the broken ceiling to which they saw. Sophia once again gave him a look, and once again Slime-Boy told her, "Sorry,"

"What about the machine?" Green asked them curiously.

"Oh, crackers," Sophia said.

They both heard something powering up outside the room; it was the machine! They all ran towards the machine, they noticed Professor Pencil was about to put his head inside the machine.

"No!" Sophia cried out loud. She grunted, looked back at Professor Pencil angrily, pulled out her right hand, and mentally pushed Professor Pencil through a wall.

"You did it!" Slime-Boy cried to her, "How did you do that?"

"I don't know," she told him, "but we need to destroy the machine as fast as we can, Blue splash all over that machine!"

"Right on it!" Blue replied to her.

"Good," she told him.

Blue pulled out both his hands and splashed all over the machine, but it wasn't circuiting.

"It must be waterproof!" Blue cried out loud.

"What do we do!?" Slime-Boy asked them curiously.

Sophia then looked at Green and told her, "Green, destroy the machine with your plants!"

"What?"

"Destroy the machine!" she cried to her, "If you do then you really are Plant-Woman."

Green then pulled out both of her hands, which she turned into long branches, and began destroying the machine as fast as she could while screaming.

"NO!"

Sophia, Blue, and Slime-Boy looked at Professor Pencil, who stepped back inside and was approaching them until Blue gave him a splash punch; knocking him out.

"He really is weak," said Blue.

Meanwhile back in The Land of Magnificent, The White Magician clawed Bird on his right cheek and punched him in the face. Once he looked back up at her, he spat out one of his teeth and jumped at The White Magician with his feet claws; ready to attack her once more. However, she was no longer there, and suddenly she grabbed him by his back and began hugging him as hard as she could. He groaned while she grinned.

"I really miss you Bird!" she told him, "I even miss hugging you," She pulled out her large tongue and licked him on the right side of his feathery head. Bird gasped.

She pushed her claws as hard as she could into his body. Once Bird let out a scream of agony, he put his head down and told her, "Do you also miss this witch!?" He then pulled his head back up to crush her entire face. She quickly let go of him, pulled out her hands, and grabbed her broken, bleeding nose, "You little feathery brat!" She pulled out her claws as high as she could and was about to attack him until he punched once again in the face. She groaned and once again grabbed her nose. He jumped as high as he could and was about to punch her until she caught his fist and twisted his fist. He let out a scream of agony and was pushed by her left long, pointy shoe. He once again fell down onto the floor while holding his twisted right fist. He was quickly pulled up by The White Magician, she hugged him as hard as she could. Bird groaned.

"Time for a kiss," The White Magician's lips were now on Bird's beak. His eyes were bigger while her eyes were closed, and suddenly, his eyes were closed as well.

Andrew gasped and saw he was back in his human form until he noticed he was laying down on a squishy pink thing. He stood up and saw The White Magician waving at him far away.

"Hello, Andrew!"

"Where are we?"

"In your mind, silly!" she replied back to him.

"This is my mind?"

"We're inside your brain, featherhead!"

"Listen," he told her, "I really don't want to fight anymore, and I'm sorry for everything,"

She looked down at the pink and gooey floor, then looked back up and replied to him as loudly as she could, "It's too late for that you brat!"

"Very well witch," he replied back to her, "let's fight in my goddamn mind,"

"With pleasure," She quickly hopped as fast as she could towards him while he turned back into his bird form and flew up as high as he could towards her. She had her claws while he had his fists. Once they got close to each other, they began attacking each other. The White Magician kept clawing at Bird while he kept punching at The White Magician. Suddenly, The White Magician jumped at Bird, once they landed on the slimy floor, she stabbed him on the right side of his chest with her left claw. He screamed in agony.

Once Professor Pencil woke up, he noticed he was tied up in Slime-Boy's slime by shooting it out from his right hand. He then noticed the four and asked them curiously, "What do you four want?"

"To tell you that you were about to kill many innocent people," Sophia replied.

"What?" he told her, "No, it's not a machine that could kill people, it's a machine that will turn people into geniuses like me,"

"No, she lied to you!" Sophia told him.

"No, I don't believe you," he told her, "only a real insane person would do that,"

"Isn't she already a real insane person?"

Professor Pencil gave a look, looked back at her, and told her, "If this machine really does kill, then why would she want me?"

"Because you're a scientist," she replied, 'and if she did it, we would have all been dead at the next second,"

"Who told you?" Professor Pencil asked him with a concerned look.

"Michael," she replied.

"What would he know?" he told her, "He's dead,"

"No, she's not lying," Blue told him, "He told all of us about her sinister plan,"

No words came out of the professor's mouth, he looked concerned instead until Sophia told him, "Think about it Professor Pencil, do you really think somebody as crazy as The White Magician would want to make your dreams come true?"

Bird punched The White Magician once again in her nose. She screamed in agony and began grabbing her nose with her right hand while pulling out her left claw to attack him with it. He tried avoiding her claw, however, and sadly, he got clawed three times in the chest. He screamed in agony and was suddenly punched in his beak by her. His blood began to drip down while he fell down onto the pink, gooey floor.

"You know it's time we stop fighting in your idiotic mind!" She cried to him, angrily.

Once Bird woke up, he stopped kissing The White Magician but couldn't get out. Once The White Magician woke up, she grinned and began pushing her claws as hard as she could; Andrew let out a scream of agony.

"Let me kill you for reals this time you puny little sparrow, you!"

His bones began to break once more, Bird was breathing painfully and was about to pass out from her claws crushing his bones once more until The White Magician felt someone tapping on her left shoulder. She turned her head around and was suddenly punched in the nose by Sophia!

"That's for what you're doing to my brother, witch!" Sophia told her angrily.

She sniffed out the blood, looked back at Sophia with an angry look, and noticed as well as Slime-Boy, Blue, Green, and even Professor Pencil on her side.

"You wooden traitor!" The White Magician cried to him angrily.

"If you want to kill the entire Earth," Professor Pencil told her, "next time do it yourself,"

"You know it's funny, Michael actually told me to get you," she told him.

"What?" he asked her, curious and confused.

"Yeah," she replied, "he told me he knew this great scientist who could do my machine faster than me, and I, of course, knew he was lying, I also knew this would happen."

"If you knew then why would you ask me?"

"He told me you had a mother,"

"I did,"

"Well, what if I told you, I was the one who hanged her on that bridge?"

"What," he told her while giving her a look.

"Oh yeah," she told him, "Pencil Pen, I knew all about you and your poor mother because of my cameras, so I decided to tell you to "invite" my machine while I had to build the real one. However, I had to make sure that you had joined me before you could ask your 'precious' mother! So I did what a crazy person would do, I controlled her and hanged her that day."

"Wait, so why would you do all of this?" Sophia asked her curiously.

"To fool you all," she told her, "I also knew if I had to build a machine to kill everyone including Gifts like myself and Professor Pencil and nature as well as being patient…! Someone with superhuman abilities would try to stop me, so I decided to hire a 'scientist' to build his machine while the real scientist, me, already worked on the real machine. Do you all want to know how the machine works? It's simple, all I have to do is push a button,"

"Then where is the machine, you crazy witch?" Sophia asked her curiously.

"You're standing right on it my annoying green little girl," Once she snapped her fingers, Wonderland was no longer seen, but was rather a large machine with a huge stick that would be unleashing a large beam of power. The good guys were all shocked and worried.

"NO!" Sophia cried worryingly and horrified.

The White Magician pulled out her left hand and pushed all of the good guys down onto the rough ground except for Professor Pencil. She controlled him and was now up as high as he could.

"As for you Professor Pencil, let's see what happens once I crush all your bones," she told him, "after all, I don't want you to betray me again!" She then formed her left hand into a fist and began crushing the inside of his body. He began screaming in agony while spitting out his own blood. She stopped. Once she did, he looked down and began breathing as painfully as he could.

"Any last words?" she asked him.

Once he coughed out a bit of blood, he began to laugh, "Yes actually," He looked back up to her and told her, "Burn in hell, you witch!" She gave an angry look at him and formed a fist as hard as she could; exploding Professor Pencil. All of his blood and organs like his brain, heart, and many more fell down onto the rough ground.

"Now as for you," she looked down at Bird, "I would love to leave you here but first,"

The White Magician then kicked him in the back once more as hard as she could; twisting his back, Bird let out a scream of agony and fainted, "Hope you never heal once I kill you and this whole planet," She patted him on his back as hard as she could twice and began floating up in the air with her telekinesis to get on top of her machine.

Once Sophia woke up, she noticed the blood and organs on the hard ground. Sophia let out a scream of horror, which woke up Slime-Boy, Blue, and Green. They too noticed Slime-Boy screamed as well while Blue and Green looked horrified. Sophia then heard a sinister laugh above her, she looked back up and noticed the demonic White Magician on the top of the machine.

"NO!"

Slime-Boy, Blue, and Green noticed and were shocked. Sophia then stood back up, pulled out her hand, and tried controlling The White Magician, however, and sadly she couldn't. Slime-Boy gave an angry look and stretched as far as he could into the shape of gooey, green stairs. He stopped once he reached the top of the machine.

"Ran quickly!" he groaned.

"You heard the boy," Sophia told Blue and Green, "Let's run!"

Sophia, Blue, and Green ran as fast as they could into the slippery, slimy stairs. Sophia almost fell down but thankfully Blue caught her. Once they reached the top of the machine, Slime-Boy was back onto the ground all normal and began breathing painfully.

"Slime-Boy!" Sophia cried as loud as she could.

"Sophia!"

Sophia turned around and saw her brother bleeding on the floor of the ride, "Andrew!" She ran towards him and was about to cry until he told her softly, "No, please don't cry because of me Sophia," he told her, "you three must stop her, and make sure the machine is actually destroyed,"

"What about Slime-Boy?"

"He'll be alright," he told her.

"But--"

"Sophia, please," He coughed out his blood as he was saying it, "stop the devil herself,"

Sophia sniffed out her tears, stood fully up, looked at Blue and Green, and told them, "Let's save the world and stop that demonic witch,"

"But what if we fail, Sophia?" Blue asked her curiously.

"Never say that!" she told him, "We won't fail, we will win,"

Blue and Green looked at each other, they both nodded at each other, looked at Sophia, and told her, "Let's save the world," They quickly were approaching the stairs, and once they got there, they quickly ran as fast as they could. Before they got up there, The White Magician was about to push the white button. Once they got there, they noticed.

"NO!" Sophia cried out loud.

The White Magician looked at Sophia, Blue, and Green; gave them an angry look, and was about to pull out her left hand until Sophia pulled out her right hand and mentally controlled The White Magician. She gasped. Sophia then tossed The White Magician onto another ride far away called "Radioactive". Once The White Magician landed on top of it, she gave a depressed look and screamed as angrily as she could. Many people heard it and were shocked to see The White Magician on top of the ride.

"What have I done!" Sophia cried worryingly.

"We saved the world, Sophia," Blue told her.

"No, those innocent people!" she replied to him, "She's going to kill them because of me!"

They both looked concerned, looked at each other, looked back at Sophia, and told her, "You need to fly us there as fast as you can!"

"Me?" she asked them curiously, "Why?"

"Because you have the ability to move objects," he told her, "you can possibly move us as well,"

"But I don't know how to control my powers!" she told him. She then grabbed her face and looked depressed and angry at the same time until she heard, "Then control them," She looked back at him with a confused face, "Huh?"

"You heard me, control them,"

"We believe in you, Sophia," Green told her.

But what if I can't!" she cried to her.

"Andrew and Slime-Boy would believe in you if they were here,"

Sophia then looked back to "Radioactive" She pulled out her right hand and tried as hard as she could to control them until she cried out, "I can't!"

"Then let me help you,"

Sophia, Blue, and Green looked on their right and saw Andrew as well as Slime-Boy!

"Andrew!" Sophia cried in happiness, "Slime-Boy! How are you two alright?"

"Let's just say I woke up," Slime-Boy replied to her, "and once I woke up, I stretched as fast as I could to get on top of the machine, and once I noticed your brother, I gave him a good kick on his chest, which healed his back."

"That's amazing," she replied to him. She then looked at Andrew, and Andrew told her, "Now little sister, let's save the world,"

Sophia and Slime-Boy were on Andrew's back while Blue and Green were holding his legs. He flew as fast as he could, he almost fell down onto the rough ground, but luckily he didn't. Once they reached the top of the ride, they noticed The White Magician was controlling a coaster filled with many innocent people. They screamed as loud as they could in horror. The White Magician was about to kill them one by one until Andrew yelled to her, "STOP!" while pulling up his right hand. She noticed and was annoyed to see them, she then told the entire group, "You may have stopped me from killing the earth, but you won't stop me from killing these people!"

"Oh, I think we will, White Magician," he replied.

"Then save them right now!" She then threw them as hard as she could, the people were screaming in horror.

"NO!" Bird and Sophia cried out loud while Slime-Boy, Blue, and Green looked concerned. The Bird then told the group, "I get the people, you stop White Magician!"

"Got it!" they all replied back to him.

The Bird flew down as high as he could to get the people, and luckily he did while The White Magician jumped to another side where the group was and began attacking them with her claws. They tried avoiding her deadly claws, Blue formed a fist and turned it as big as it could get and was about to punch her hard in the left side of her face until she was no longer there, and suddenly he could feel deadly claws piercing his back. He breathed painfully, Green tried punching her with her large, super fist until she turned invisible and clawed Green all over her body and pushed her down and was about to fall down onto the rough ground until Bird caught her and was beginning to fly back up. Sophia and Slime-Boy jumped as high as they could, formed a fist on their hands, and were about to punch her until she disappeared, which made both Sophia and Slime-Boy knocking each other by accident. They both fell down onto the wooden floor, Sophia was then mentally moved by The White Magician once more.

"Tell me something Sophia," she told her, "do you like to see the inside of your body? Because I'm about to pull out all of your insides!" She formed a fist as hard as she could, Sophia's body felt odd, almost as if her insides were about to come out of her body; she let out a scream in agony. The White Magician grinned, "At least something good came out of this!" Suddenly, she felt somebody tapping her shoulders on her left side, she turned her head behind and was punched in the nose by both Bird and Green. She let out a scream of agony and once again grabbed her own bloody nose.

"It's time me and my friends end your reign of terror, White Magician,"

"Oh but, I don't think so, Andrew," she replied to him. She jumped at them, punched Green in the face, and once they were on the floor, she began hugging Andrew as hard as she could. Bird groaned.

"I will crush you this time, sparrow!" The White Magician cried to him. She pushed her hands as hard as she could; he coughed out blood while The White Magician was laughing as crazily as she could be until she was mentally pushed by Sophia herself! Sophia then mentally controlled her and was now as high as she could. Sophia walked towards her brother, Andrew, who muttered to her while smiling, "I knew you could do it... I always knew," She smiled back at him. Once she looked back to The White Magician, she began taking backward steps, and once she was done, she controlled The White Magician to be close to her, "Now let's see how you feel with your insides!" She formed a fist as hard as she could in her right hand, and The White Magician herself groaned; she could feel the pain inside of her body. When a minute passed, suddenly, The White Magician began to laugh as crazily as she could, looked back at Sophia, and told her, "Do it,"

"I will!"

A minute has passed, and yet nothing.

"DO IT!" She cried to her as loudly as she could.

Sophia looked down at the wooden floor, and once another minute had passed, she looked back at her with a grin and told her, "With pleasure witch!" She was forming her fast as hard as she could while The White Magician groaned and laughed crazily at the same time.

"Sophia, stop!"

Sophia gasped, she looked back down at her brother, Andrew with a depressed look on his face, she looked back up at The White Magician, who had a grin on her face.

"Please, don't do this," he told her.

She closed her eyes and began to think until she knew what to do, she first looked down at Andrew with a smile, Andrew smiled back at her. Sophia then looked at The White Magician, moved close to her, and told her, "Have fun in prison, witch!" She then tossed her mentally down inside a food stand. She crashed down onto the popcorn, she even spat out popcorn out of her mouth while the police approached her armed with guns. She began to laugh as crazily as ever for one last time.

Meanwhile back on the top of Radioactive, Sophia fell down to the wooden floor and began breathing as heavily as she could.

"I knew you could do it, Sophia," Andrew told her, "I'm so proud of you, and our dad would be too," He smiled.

"Thanks, Andrew," She replied while smiled back at him, "I can't wait to tell our father about this,"

They both laughed, and then Andrew asked her curiously, "Should we wake everyone up?"

"I think we should," replied Sophia.

Once they woke everyone up, Bird told everyone what Sophia did, and they were thrilled at what they heard. They all hugged her as fast as they could, and when they stopped hugging her, Slime-Boy asked her curiously, "How did you control your powers, Sophia?"

"I don't know, I was just angry and I began to control her,"

"Sophia, that's it!" Andrew told her.

"What?"

"Your emotions and actions," he told her, "Whenever you feel angry or sad or heroic, you can control your own telekinesis,"

"Awesome, Andrew," she replied, "what do we do now with all those people?"

"Yeah those people are going to fear us," said Slime-Boy.

Blue and Green looked at each other with a worried look.

'I know what to do," Andrew told them, "we tell them the truth, well not the entire truth, we'll tell them our nicknames and who was truly responsible for this sinister act,"

"That's really smart Andrew!" Sophia cried to him.

"Everybody get a hold of me," he told them.

Once Bird flew down onto the rough ground with his friends, there was a whole crowd of people including police officers. The people gasped while the police officers pulled out their guns and told them, "Freeze freaks!"

"I'll show you a freak!" Radioactive-Girl cried to him.

"Radioactive-Girl, no," Bird told her after he pulled out his arm to stop her.

Radioactive-Girl nodded back at him and looked back at the people, who gasped once more.

"For those of you who don't know me my name is Bird," he told the people, "and these are my friends. Tonight was supposed to be the park's anniversary but instead, you sadly got to see that both superheroes and supervillains are real… we are not the villains, the real monster here is The White Magician, who Radioactive-Girl successfully defeated all by herself with her telekinesis. We are not here to harm you, we are here for today to protect you, and if you want us to be taken away by the authorities, then we will be taken away.

"NO!" cried all the people but the police officers.

"You saved us from that insane rabbit!" cried a man.

"You guys were heroic and brave!" cried a woman.

"Please don't take them away officers!" cried a child.

Suddenly, all the people chanted to the police, "Don't take them away!" as many times as they could until the chief said, "They're right, these guys really did save our butts… drop your guns, all of you,"

"Yes, chief,"

"Right away!"

All the police officers began dropping their guns as the people began clapping and cheering for the superheroes. Suddenly, an anchorwoman entered the crowd and got close to the heroes with her cameraman. Once she introduced herself she asked them, "Who are you guys?"

"I'm Bird,"

"Radioactive-Girl,"

"The Waterman,"

"Plant-Woman,"

"And I'm Slime-Boy,"

"Do you guys have a name?" the anchorwoman asked them curiously.

They looked at each other and then formed a circle. Once they were done talking, Bird told the anchorwoman, "As a matter of fact we do, The Saviours,"

"Thank you, Saviours," replied the anchorwoman nicely.

The people including the police began to clap and cheer for the heroes of today, The Saviours!

VII

The Aftermath

What was now number one on trending was a group of superheroes called The Saviours. For tonight, they were The Saviours of Forest City! Bird explained more on The White Magician to the anchorwoman including her own sinister plan. The Waterman and Plant-Woman also informed the anchorwoman about Michael E, the one who freed them, Radioactive-Girl, and Slime-Boy when they were captured by The White Magician herself. Radioactive-Girl and Slime-Boy also informed the anchorwoman about Professor Pencil like he was a Gift like The White Magician to be tricked and killed by The White Magician herself. The world was truly never going to be the same ever again. It's what Bird said that tonight was supposed to be the park's 50th anniversary but instead the people got a glimpse of both Superheroes and Supervillains.

Once Andrew and Sophia returned to the forest; they returned to the treehouse and saw their poor father still in the bed. He had been drinking about four water bottles, two from yesterday and two from today. Once their father noticed his children, he smiled and told them, "You came back!"

"Yes, father," they both replied to him.

"Did you and your new friends ever defeat that evil fireman?" the father asked them curiously.

The two gave a look and looked at each other; the father gave a worried and confused look. Once the two looked back at him, Sophia told him, "It's a really long story dad,"

"Tomorrow we'll tell you," said Andrew.

"In the house because my back is still broken,"

"Oh yeah," Sophia told him, "about your back, I'm so sorry I broke it,"

"It's alright Sophia," he told her, "I know you didn't mean to my little girl," Once he touched the right side of her face, covering up her tears, she smiled and hugged him, he hugged her back with a smile while Sophia began crying. Andrew then joined the family hug.

Once they got back home with the help from Andrew's wings, the father noticed Blue, Green, and Slime-Boy. Andrew informed him that Slime-Boy would be staying tonight as for Blue and Green, they would be staying up in the attic, his father agreed. Everyone cheered and it was now time to go to bed until Sophia (who was no longer wearing her uniform but was wearing normal clothing) heard a knock on the bedroom door. She stood up and walked as slowly as she could, and when she answered it, she saw Slime-Boy.

"Hi," Slime-Boy told her.

"Oh, what do you want, Slime-Boy?"

"Jason,"

"What?"

"My name is Jason Woods,"

Once she smiled, she told him, "That's a handsome name,"

"Why thank you, Sophia Smith," he then pulled out his right, slimy hand. Once she noticed she pulled out her right, glowing hand and shook his slimy hand, "It's so good to finally meet you,"

"You too Jason,"

He quickly hugged her, and she quickly hugged him back. They both smiled at each other.

One Day Later

"So, let me get this straight," said Andrew and Sophia's father, "The White Magician was behind it all, she tricked all of you and almost killed the entire Earth. As for Michael, he was not really a bad guy but was instantly killed by her and so was Professor Pencil. You were all revealed by the public, you two and your new friends are now the new Saviours. Oh, and she watched an entire city with her cameras this entire time including whenever we go to the bathroom,"

"Pretty much yeah, dad," replied Andrew.

"Jesus," he said.

"But we stopped her in the end," Sophia told him, "that's all that matters,"

"For now," he replied to her, "what happens if she gets out of the asylum?"

"If she gets out, we'll be ready," Andrew told him.

10:30 AM

"Are you guys sure this is a good idea?" Jason Light asked the three.

"Jason this is the only way," Sophia replied to him.

Once Jason took a deep breath, he told her, "Alright, here goes nothing... oh and sorry for the mess,"

"That's all right Jason," replied the father of Andrew and Sophia, "I can clean up the slime out of my car,"

Before Jason stepped outside of their father's vehicle, Jason gave both Andrew and Sophia a big hug while telling them, "Thank you for everything!" They hugged him back while their father smiled. Once Jason, Andrew, Sophia stepped outside his vehicle while he was going to park it and met them later inside the house. Once they approached a small house, Jason rang the doorbell once, they heard a teenage female's voice saying, "I'll get it!" Once the person ran down the stairs and opened the door; revealing it to be a thirteen-year-old girl with light brown hair and dark brown eyes, "Holy...! You're them!"

"You know who we are already?" Slime-Boy asked her curiously.

"Of course, you're The Saviours!"

"Oh, that," he replied to her.

"Although, I don't see Waterman or Plant-Woman," She then looked at the with a curious and confused look, "Why are you guys here,"

"Hello Abby," Slime-Boy told her.

"How do you know my name?" she asked him, horrified.

"Look at my eyes and tell me who I am,"

Once she looked at him eye to eye, she noticed his eyes were as brown as hers. She was shocked as she recognized those eyes to be, "Jason?"

"Good to see you, big sister."

Abby Woods quickly gave her little brother a big hug, grabbed him, and told him while sobbing, "I missed you so much!"

"I miss you too Abby," he patted her on her shoulder, "you don't care that I'm all slimy?"

Once she stopped hugging him, she put him back down and told him, "Of course not, you're my little brother. I would never care what you look like." He smiled and quickly gave her a big hug. She hugged him back and smiled as well while Andrew and Sophia smiled.

"Abby, who's in the door?" her father asked her curiously. Once he walked towards her, he was about to ask her again until he noticed him, "Andrew?"

"Hello Charles," he told him, "my dear old friend,"

Sophia gave Andrew a confused look until Andrew told her, "Sophia this is Charles Woods, the founder of Freedom," Sophia was shocked and looked back at Charles, who was smiling.

"Come here, my old friend!" he pulled out his hands and Andrew hugged him, "I missed you indeed!"

"I miss you too Charles," he replied.

"So, this must be your little sister, Sophia," he told her while looking at her, and told Sophia, "I heard a great story all about you,"

"Really?"

"Really,"

Once Andrew and Charles stopped hugging while Abby and Jason stopped hugging, Charles pulled out his right hand, and Sophia pulled out her glowing right hand for a good shake.

"Nice to finally meet you, Sophia," Charles Woods told her.

"You too, Charles," she smiled. She then looked at Abby. Once she stopped shaking Charles' hand, she once again pulled out her glowing, right hand and told her, "Sophia Smith," she smiled while Abby smiled as well, pulled out her slimy, right hand and shook on it, "Abby Woods,"

"Hi Dad," Jason told him.

Charles looked down and was surprised to see his son as a slimy boy. He told him, "Jason, is that really you?"

"Yes, father,"

Charles smiled and hugged Jason as quickly as he could, "Welcome back son!"

"Well, I wouldn't be back if it wasn't for Andrew, Sophia, and our other two friends,"

"Really?" Charles looked back at Andrew and Sophia and told them, "Thank you for taking good care of my son,"

"It wasn't easy at first," Sophia told him.

Andrew chuckled while Charles looked back at him and asked him curiously, "Where's your father, Andrew?"

"Oh, he's coming,"

"Good because I would like to have a word with him," he told him, "in the meantime, come in you two,"

Once they got inside, Andrew and Sophia were talking to Charles while Abby was with her little brother, Jason in their basement.

'So tell me, Andrew," Charles told him, "How had you been doing before last night?"

"I've been doing good with my little sister, Sophia,"

"How's your father?"

"He's good right now," he told him, "I had to fix his back last night with my super strength,"

"Really?"

"Yes," he told him, "and it took almost forever for me to push back in his body,"

"That must have sounded exhausting,"

"Oh, it was,"

They all laughed until Andrew asked him, "How have you been doing?"

"Not good,"

"How come?"

"My wife got into a car accident last year,"

"Oh yes," he told him, "I'm so sorry to hear that,"

"It's alright, Andrew," he told him, "it's not your fault… is the devil really locked up in The Loony Bin?"

"The White Magician is in the police department for now," he told him, "until her court day arrives, and let's hope she gets transferred into The Loony Bin for the rest of her life because those two didn't deserve to die,"

"Let's just hope that witch is finally locked up in a place where she truly belongs,"

Meanwhile with Jason and Abby,

"What are we doing in your laboratory, Abby?" Jason asked her curiously.

"I brought you here because I might have found a cure for you,"

"What do you mean?" he asked her curiously.

"What I mean is," she told him, "I might have found a cure on how to turn you back to human,"

Jason was shocked, and was confused, to which he asked her curiously, "I thought you said you didn't care what I looked like?"

"I don't little brother, but what about you?" she asked him, "Do you care about your body…?" Once she walked towards him, she told him, "And Jason, please don't lie to me,"

Meanwhile back with Andrew, Sophia, and Charles. They heard the doorbell ring.

"I'll get it," Charles told them. Once he answered the door, he saw Andrew and Sophia's father outside his front door, "My old friend!"

"Good to see you too Charles,"

Charles hugged him, and he hugged him back.

"Good to see you indeed," Charles told him.

Once their father got inside, Charles asked him curiously, "How have you been doing, my old friend?"

"I'm doing good,"

"Would you two please visit Abby and Jason in the basement?" Charles told Andrew and Sophia, "We're about to have a talk that only grownups would understand,"

"Alright Charles," Andrew told him.

"Of course," Sophia told him.

Once they went down the basement, Charles told him, "How have you been my friend since the last time we saw each other?"

"Not well," he weeping beneath his right eye.

"I feel your pain, my friend," he told him, "I too have lost my true love,"

"What is it that you really want to talk about?" he asked him, "It's definitely not about The White Magician, since that devil is going to asylum."

"I have found it,"

"Found what?"

Charles gave him a look, and once he realized, he asked him curiously, "Are you sure?"

Once Charles stood up from his chair, he told his friend, "Follow me upstairs then,"

Meanwhile back with Andrew and Sophia, once they reached down the basement. Andrew was amazed at what he was seeing, a laboratory while Sophia was not excited but was rather annoyed. They then noticed Jason and Abby talking to each other.

"Jason!" Sophia cried to him happily.

Once Jason and Abby noticed them, Jason yelled out to her in excitement, "Sophia!" The two ran towards each other and hugged as quickly as they could with a smile. Andrew and Abby slowly approached them, and once they did, Andrew looked up at Abby and told her with a smile, "My name is Andrew Luck," He then pulled out his right brown feather, "I really like your laboratory, Abby," She smiled, pulled out her right hand and shook his hand while telling him, "My name is Abby Woods, and thank you, I really like your attitude, Andrew."

December 25th
Christmas Day
The Loony Bin

"Hey, rabbit!" A guard yelled at her, "You've got a guest,"

The White Magician already knew who it was before Bird himself stepped inside her white room.

"Hello old friend," he told her.

She looked away from him and looked back at the puffy wall.

"I have a present for you,"

"Is it a book?" she told him, "And I didn't even have to read your mind, because if I did I would have already been tased by this stupid ankle bracelet the police put on my left foot."

"Please," he told her, "I just want to talk,"

She sighed, The White Magician looked back at him and sat down while Bird sat down at another seat. Once he gave The White Magician her present, she quickly unwrapped it; revealing it to be a classical book "Alice Adventures in Wonderland" She chuckled, looked back at Bird, and told him, "Are you joking?"

"You have only seen the Disney version," he told her, "it's time you've read the actual book,"

"Do you really think I'll be locked up here for the rest of my life?" she asked him curiously.

"I don't know White," he told her, "if you try espacing, then me and my friends will stop you once more,"

"Ha!" she shouted to him, "Yeah right, you may have won the fight Bird, but the war has yet to begun,"

"Tell me something White," he told her, "How have you been doing before we saw each other again and before your demonic plan?"

"Not well, really," she told him.

The White Magician began to weep beneath her left eye.

"What's the matter White?" he asked her curiously, "You've seen to be depressed than your usual self,"

"It's just when I truly grow up," she told him, "I wouldn't be able to love you ever again until you turn eighteen as well. I might be crazy Bird, but I'm not a sick person,"

He chuckled and told her, "Good to know,"

"Tell me something sparrow," she told him, "do you ever wonder if something bad would happen to you and your friends including Radioactive-Girl? Now that you and your friends are officially Superheroes while I'm a Supervillain,"

"Every night," he told her, "I always have bad dreams about one of us dying from a heroic act,"

"Exactly," she told him, "just because your superheroes doesn't mean you and your friends will always be lucky in life, including me,"

"I will make sure nothing bad always happens to my group," he told her, "because if you dare touch any of them including Radioactive-Girl, I swear to god, I will not go so easy on you,"

"Times up, you two!" The guard cried to them, he opened the door, and once Bird stepped outside, The White Magician pushed her small table as hard as she could, and began running towards him but the technological door quickly locked itself. She groaned and accidentally hit her nose, it began to bleed. The guard laughed at her and told her, "Nice try!" before walking away. Before Bird could walk away, The White Magician shouted to him, "You won't think things will be easy next time! Next time I'm going to kill you and everyone you ever loved including your dumb friends you stupid sparrow! When I get out of here, and I will get out, I'm going to kill him and her! You hear me! I'M GOING TO KILL HIM AND HER!"

Meanwhile back in 123 Pine Street,

"Here you go, Sophia, I got this one just for you!" Jason told her.

"Thanks, Jason," replied Sophia (whose skin was back to normal because Sophia could now control her body) Once she unwrapped it, she opened the box; revealing it to be a basketball.

"A basketball?" Sophia told him.

"You told me you liked sports," he replied to her, "and your that your favorite sport was basketball so I decided to buy you a basketball."

"Jason," she told him. "I love it!" She quickly hugged him while he hugged her back, they both smiled at each other.

"I knew you would love it, Sophia," he told her.

Once they stopped hugging, she quickly gave him his present, "Here you go, Jason."

"Thanks, Sophia," replied Jason. Once he unwrapped it, he opened the box, revealing it to be an entire collection of slime toys. Jason looked at her.

"Don't you like it?"

"No, Sophia, I don't like it," he told her, "I love it! Thank you!" He quickly hugged her once more as she once again hugged him back, they both smiled at each other one more time.

"Thank you!" he told her.

"You're welcome, my friend," she replied.

Once they heard a knock on the door, the father answered it and said, "Andrew, you finally came!" His father hugged him while he hugged him back.

"It took a while to see her,"

"And how is that devil?"

"Let's just say," he told him, "she's where she belongs,"

"Good,"

Once Andrew ran up the small stairs he greeted everyone including Blue and Green. They greeted him back. Once Andrew hugged Sophia, she gave him a present, "Here's your present, Andrew," Once Andrew grabbed it, he unwrapped it as gently as he could, he opened the box; revealing it to be a comic book called "The Adventures of Bird!"

"I thought you might love it," she smiled, "It's your first issue, I bought it the day it came,"

"Thank you, Sophia," he smiled, "and I do love it, but not as much as I love you,"

Sophia quickly got up from her sofa and hugged her big brother, Andrew as hard as she could while he hugged her little sister, Sophia back. Everyone smiled while some gave out tears of joy.

"I love you, Andrew," she told him while turning her skin green again.

"I love you too, Sophia," he told her.

Epilogue

9:00 PM

Andrew, Sophia, Jason, Blue, Green, and even Abby were watching the first Home Alone. This was Andrew and Abby's tenth time seeing the movie, it was Sophia and Jason's third time seeing the movie, and it was Blue and Green's first time seeing the movie. They were all laughing until the channel was interrupted, "We interrupt this program for some breaking news," said the newswoman, "Tonight, a woman dressed up as an ant inside of a robotic ant is attacking the L.A.B.S. building. Here's our anchorwoman, Jessica in the scene, Jessica,"

"Thank you, Emma," Jessica told her, and then told everyone, "Tonight, a crazy woman is attacking the L.A.B.S. building. Let's take a good look at her, Jimmy."

Once her cameraman, Jimmy, pointed at the crazy woman in the ant costume, they could hear her saying, "I am The Ant Queen…! Feel my wrath as I destroy one of your famous buildings in this large city, and then Forest City itself!"

The Saviours and Abby noticed what was happening. Once The Saviours stood up, Andrew looked at his group and told them, "Looks like Home Alone would have to wait for another time, Sophia, I need you to go to the bathroom and put your suit on as fast as you can while the rest go outside with me." he then looked back at Sophia and told her, "And Sophia once your done, I need you to meet us outside the house," he finally told his entire team, "Once we're outside, Blue, Green, and Jason you must run as fast as you can if you want to catch up to us, as for you Sophia, fly with me, and remember we must the people inside and outside the building, and stop The Ant Queen before she attacks the city itself, got it?"

"Got it," the rest of the team told him.

Everyone but Sophia was outside after saying, "See you later, Abby!" while Sophia was up in the bathroom putting on her suit. Once she was done, she ran down the stairs and told Abby, "See you later, Abby!" and shut the door as quickly as she could. Once they were all outside, both Andrew and Sophia were up in the air, Andrew flying while Sophia was using her telekinesis while Blue, Green, and Jason were running as fast as they could. Once they approached the building, Andrew noticed The Ant Queen, who noticed her, and punched her in the face!

The End

To Yolanda Guerra
"A Beloved Mother as well as A Great Friend"

My History

My name Is Arturo Lopez Jr. and I was born on September 23, 2003. I was born in the state of California; in the city of San Jose. My parents were from Santa Ana Maya, Mexico. I was the first in my family to be born in America. I don't remember much from my past as a baby, however, I do remember my past as a small child. I don't know if I ever went to a preschool or not, I do know that I went to an elementary school named Edenvale. On my first day, I went to kindergarten and I was so sad to see my mom leave me that I always cried whenever she dropped me off there. I luckily graduated kindergarten and moved on to first grade and on to sixth grade. Sixth grade was the last grade for my elementary school. I was sad to leave my old school, however, I was also happy going to a new school, middle school. However, before I talk about my middle school days, I would like to talk about my Boys & Girls Club days. When me and my little brother were small children, our parents took us to a wonderful place called the Boys & Girls Club. There I met new friends, they weren't exactly my age, however, they were the best of friends I ever had in my whole life. Whenever I came there, I would always have fun drawing or doing more fun stuff. Sadly, I stopped going there because I no longer felt I was at the right age to go there. In the end, all the friends I once knew left the place and went to other jobs and have happy lives. Back in my middle school days, after I graduated from elementary school and had a wonderful summer, I went to my middle school, Davis. I met two wonderful friends, one of them was my girlfriend, however, and sadly, that didn't last so long though. I'm not really a person who would have a lot of friends, the only true best friend I ever had in my life was Porfirio from an old summer school I used to go to. I also have another friend from my life, his name is Jorge and he was indeed one of the best of friends I have ever met and his mom was as kind as an angel. After I graduated from middle school, I moved on to my high school, Oak Grove. Right now I've graduated High School. Once I went to high school, I was met with mixed feelings. My first year was great! My second was depressing. My third and fourth had the involvement of Covid-19. If you don't know what Covid-19 is, if you're probably reading this in the year 2031 or another year then Covid-19 was one of the worst things to ever happen to our planet earth. This made us go to lockdowns, made us go to school online rather than remotely, and much worse. Hopefully, Covid-19 will end, since I'm writing this in the year 2021. When I finished high school, I began writing my book this summer. However, I could talk about my family. First is my brother Brandon, he's basically my first friend, back then we used to fight but he is one of the best people I have ever met in my whole life. Second is my only sister, Bryanna, at first we were enemies to each other, however, we became really good friends in the end. The third is my second and little brother, Kevin, he is a lot of fun and makes adorable noises whenever he appears and is indeed considered as one of my friends. Fourth is my mother, Demetria she is honestly the best mother I ever had in my whole life, she tells me what to do, cooks my meals, folds my clothing, does cleaning while the fifth is my father, Arturo who is honestly the best father I ever had in my whole life, he takes me to stores, buys whatever I want and they both love me even when I'm acting childish in front of them.

Now that you know about my life, it's time that I tell you about the history I had with this book you recently finished reading. It all began back in my middle school days where I made a comic book about Water Man fighting three tree people. The story was about a Water Man trying to save the lives of his parents from the evil tree people. Originally, Water Man was just a human being exposed to toxic waste and water, turning him into a

Water Man! I sadly lost the comic book, and won't tell you what the rest of the plot is. I then came up with a bird superhero. I started writing many books, but they all failed except for one, The Savers. It was originally called that until I found out that it meant money. So I quickly changed the title to The Saviours and kept the story. I first thought it was a stupid story, so I decided to rewrite the entire book in the summer and completed it by July 15, 2021. That's my history, for now, I hoped you enjoyed it!

Printed in the United States
by Baker & Taylor Publisher Services